I *Swear*
It Wasn't
Me!

VALLENTINA TURMINA

I Swear It Wasn't Me!

BASED ON A TRUE STORY

livr(a)

Edited by *Ane Costa*
Cover art by *Alyssa Cirelli*
Layout by *Larissa Chagas*

Editora Livr(a)
editoralivra.com

"In keeping silent about evil, in burying it so deep within us that no sign of it appears on the surface, we are implanting it, and it will rise up a thousand fold in the future. When we neither punish nor reproach evildoers, we are not simply protecting their trivial old age, we are thereby ripping the foundations of justice from beneath new generations."

ALEKSANDR I. SOLZHENITSYN

This book is for my "bisnonna" Angelina
Fassina Tomazi, a wise woman with the
most beautiful smile in the world. She
believed everyone deserves justice and
made sure everyone around her had a
voice. Thank you for everything!

*Point your camera to this QR Code and listen to
this novel's soundtrack on Spotify.*

Author's note

A wise person once told me that if you are going to tell the truth, you have to tell the whole truth. You shouldn't hide your wrongdoings or character flaws when telling the truth because then it is not the truth, but your own opinion of the truth. Therefore, this story is fiction because the truth cannot be fully told. Now the reader is left to wonder what is true and what came from my imagination. Happy reading!

Contents

Foreword *14*

The Beginning *17*

Day 1 - Trial *36*

Farm - Yellowhammer *81*

Here Now *108*

Day 4 - Judgment *115*

The Verdict *134*

Foreword

"The truth has fiction structure"
Jacques Lacan

I choose to begin this preface by quoting the psychoanalyst Jacques Lacan about how life presents itself as fiction to ourselves. The human species has the power to create and develop stories.

This fiction, this fantasy that is our life narrative, will accompany us eternally.

Curious to think that no single human being is better off alone than a chimpanzee in a forest until today. We are fragile. Yuval Harari in Sapiens says that language and the power to tell - and believe—stories made us control the planet. We are the only species that can collaborate flexibly and in large numbers simultaneously.

Think about ants: ants can't reinvent their social system overnight. There is a hierarchy in the anthill, an m.o. Dolphins and chimpanzees even collaborate, but not in large numbers like ants. The only animal that can combine the two is WE, humans. Because we are the only species inscribed in language with the unique ability to imagine. To tell stories, myths— religions, political, and financial systems. And our own personal fictional narrative - the stories we tell about ourselves.

This articulation differentiates us from animals by our power to imagine. We can relate and dominate because we can invent narratives and convince others to believe them. Because we are inscribed in language, we can move the world through shared fiction.

Our fantasy is our way of existing in the world. From our private fiction, we establish shared fictions: nations, money, religions, government, and political ideologies. We exist from and because of this: fantasy. It is our mark on language, and it is a uniquely human ability. We use language not only to describe reality but to create new realities.

Vallentina's novella, *I swear it wasn't me*, transports us to a world of realness within fiction. She creates distinct new worlds. The way the author introduces us to relatives, judges, and characters is real to the point where we question if this is fiction or non-fiction. Her compelling writing and extraordinary talent as a narrator-character transport us to San Francisco, Florida, and everywhere else she guides us. Vallentina develops the conflicts, narrates with highly developed characterization, and reminds us to question whether life is a great piece of fiction. Aren't we all characters in someone else's story? Aren't we characters of our very own narrative and stories we tell about ourselves every day? How many times have you convinced yourself in other to convince others: *I swear it wasn't me* embraces this journey of self-discovery. It's a must-read.

Maytê Carvalho.

Marketeer, winner of Brazil's The Apprentice Special
Edition, best-selling author, currently serving as the
Chief Growth & Strategy Officer at Cubo, NYC.

Chapter One

The Beginning

This story is very different from what you've read in the newpapers.

This is my version of the facts of how I became a crime star, an icon of evil, the bogey-girl of the U.S. The disturbing thing about this story is not just the crimes they accuse me of, but the portrait media has done of me. They call me "The Evil Daughter," "The Killer Girl," and "Florida Cancer." These are pretty perverse adjectives for a girl of only sixteen; if people believe I'm innocent, of course. Teenagers don't usually make great evil crime geniuses.

It all started when I was only thirteen. At that age, my greatest worry was my first kiss, where it would take place, and who would be the lucky person. I went to school and tried to keep my grades up. So I guess God must have found my life very boring and decided to mess things up, and when I least expected it, everything turned upside down. A hurricane hit me. I named it Hurricane Nora. I gave it my name because, in general, hurricanes' names have nothing to do with their emergence. It's a random choice, but despite being tired of repeating that I have nothing to do with what happened, for them, I am the cause, effect, and proportion of the disaster. I am the one to blame.

It turns out that I am the most affected by Hurricane "Nora," in addition to not being responsible for its emergence. I am in the eye of chaos. And whoever is close to me is certainly not in the best place either. One way or another, everyone who comes just a bit closer to me will pay the price.

But I want to declare that I'm not the criminal or evil incarnate, as everyone says. I'm just another teenager in the century of the depressed. I know that the world has become a complicated place, that life has become a sea of the undertow and a dangerous place where the truth is a rare commodity. But there has to be a place inside of us where we can overcome tyranny, hatred, resentment, and exploitation of others for our own benefit. There needs to be a good place inside of us where there is room for justice to flourish, where we can face each other without suspecting that in a hug, there can be hands that hold daggers. An injustice done to someone is not an injustice to just one person. It is an injustice to everyone. Today I may be wrongly accused and convicted, but if people don't care, tomorrow, it could be someone else.

A lie repeated several times about the same person might one day be accepted as the truth. I learned it in the most painful way from my own family. Not always the ones who put us to sleep, rock us when we are crying as a baby, or "raise" us are really on our side. As for me, a game of appearances consolidates cruelty into "love" for the world and aggression for myself. The worst thing about it is silence. No one believes me, no one can hear me scream, and no one can know about my suffering. That's the traditional way; I am silenced in the name of good customs, the perverse heritage of authoritarian regimes that passed from father to son, perpetuating attitudes that causes fear. Whoever causes more fear, whether by brute force, cursing, or the old "corrective" measures that, when punishing, always carry with them the excuse to educate, is the game's winner. Sometimes, when someone is rocking a child to stop crying, they might be more interested in their ears' benefit rather than relieving the crying baby's hunger or discomfort.

My story goes through three traumatic events. The first is the death of my parents. I was with them when it happened; they were with me for one minute, and the next, they were gone. The second is the death of my uncle John. He was killed on his farm in Alabama. And the third is the death of my grandparents. A gas leak. Of these three tragedies, the first one, I can't understand what happened. I don't know if there is a culprit. The second I suspect who is to blame, I can list several reasons they would do that. And the third, for me, was a fatality, an accident.

But guess what? Taking advantage of loopholes in the law, some prosecutors and lawmakers in Alabama thought it was a good idea to put me on trial as an adult. That would be bad enough, but it turns out that there are cases where the accused has already entered the courtroom with their sentence carved in stone. Corruption cases are only increasing, and several prosecutors, judges, and prison directors are part of a scheme that basically boils down to this: The more young people arrested, the more public money going into private penitentiaries. It is not difficult to do this calculation. In my case, they saw an opportunity and took action. It turns out that they did not count on my accusations gaining so much notoriety, the repercussion of my case was immense, and that must be bad for business.

So if someone asks what I should expect from all this, I won't be able to answer them. The media is fired up over a macabre case, accusing me, while institutionalized criminals are balancing protecting their scheme with my designation that can solve their problems or destroy them. And I, amid this crossfire, feel like I've already lost. Even if I get acquitted, there's no way I can get back what they took from me.

Imagine this scenario: a young woman loses her parents. Then, she is sent to live with her paternal relatives, and when she gets there, she discovers that she ended up in the worst place in the world. She starts to be humiliated and exploited. One day, another tragedy happens—a murder. Someone kills her uncle, and everyone begins to suspect she is to blame. They accuse her... And then they send her away.

That's when she goes to live with her maternal grandparents. The explorations end, but another type of violence begins. Her grandfather attacks her, calls her every bad name in the book, berates, punches, kicks, smacks her, and gives her humiliating punishments. The kind of punishment she can't bare say out loud or write it down; punishments not even therapists and psychiatrists can handle without a pitiful look on their faces. What happened in that house was never a one-time thing, it was constant, and her grandmother pretended not to see it. Then after a few months of this, her grandparents die on a random morning, an accident and another tragedy in the young woman's life. People suspect that maybe it was her all along. She doesn't know where to go. They start an investigation on her, formalize the accusations, the press begins reporting it, and she goes from a victim to a criminal in a blink of an eye.

Nonsense, right?

I thought I had lost everything when two unexpected gifts came to my rescue. My uncles Ted and Mark arrived when I didn't know what else to do or where to go.

I was finally in a good place when they rescued me after my grandparents died.

I feel that only now I've come to understand what I've lived. I couldn't get an exact dimension of what was going on as I went through it all. Here with my uncles, I have affection, respect, and genuine care. Life with Uncles Ted and Mark is an oasis in the desert. They help me overcome traumas and losses and will be by my side at the hearings that will happen soon. They pay for the lawyer's costs, my medication, and therapy; they take care of me. But most importantly, they don't see me as a criminal.

We live in a small apartment in San Francisco, California. The apartment belongs to Uncle Ted, my mother's younger brother. Uncle Ted lived his entire childhood with my mother in Florida, but when he was about my age, he came out to my grandfather and got kicked out of the house. My grandfather was strict, conservative, authoritarian, and aggressive, especially when he was drunk. The problem is he was frequently drunk, so it was very difficult to be at ease around him. I know what I'm talking about—I was often beaten when I lived with him and my grandmother. He hurt me when things didn't go as he demanded, when I didn't answer his requests, or even for no reason, just out of habit.

Uncle Ted says he knows what my grandfather was capable of. When he was a child, he would get beaten up by his father, who used to tell him to "man up." I can feel his pain when he talks about my grandfather. I can feel how hard it is for him—a pain even worse than the physical one, a stain he carries to this day.

Uncle Ted came to California alone. He established himself here without anyone's help. But for that, he had to face harsh experiences. He was without family, without friends, without anything. He slept a few days on the street, starved, and even had to become a prostitute. He became vulnerable and increasingly distant from everything and everyone he knew. After he left Florida, he never had contact with anyone else in the family. He only heard about me from the news, and that's when he decided to look for me.

I knew my mother had a brother. But the version of the story she told me about him was quite different. According to her, he had run away from home, disappeared, and they could never find him. After a while, they stopped looking for him because they thought he was dead. Turns out my mother never mentioned anything about my grandfather, about his troubled relationship with Uncle Ted. I could see that this subject was difficult for her, a real taboo. But the few times my mother let slip something about her missing brother, she recalled stories of them with great affection. She recalled them playing in the old house's basement, how she helped her mother take care of and educate uncle Ted, always mentioning how bright he was.

For my uncle Ted, my mother was a role model. When they were children, he copied everything she did to be like her. He thought she was beautiful; he wanted to wear her clothes and play with her toys; he idolized his sister. I guess Uncle Ted saw in mom the representation of a mother figure. After all, she was the one who took care of him when grandma couldn't. She was his world when he was a kid, and after they got older, they were great friends and lived close together. Uncle Ted says my mother was the first person he told he was gay. She knew everything about him, his passions and secrets, and he knew everything about her. Uncle Ted says the hardest thing for him was not leaving his parent's house; instead, it was saying goodbye to his sister, my mother. She was the only good thing he had in his life, so losing her meant losing everything.

I suspect that maybe it's because of this affection towards my mother that he rescued me. After all, who would open their door to a person accused of murdering their own family? Who would want to be around a girl that only caused disasters wherever she went? Who would want the hurricane "Nora" in their lives? Nobody! And that's why my uncles are either crazy or they actually believe me.

I prefer to go with the second option. Having my uncles on my side and trusting me means I can trust them too.

I know my being here is a challenging situation for them. I completely changed their lives. Even shopping became something weird—we walk into a supermarket and feel the eyes surrounding us, mothers pulling their children away from us in fear, cashiers who seem scared of us... It's not easy! I feel like a freak.

I was used to how people treated me, but it was all new to my uncles. They didn't know how to take care of or deal with someone new in their lives—especially because that new someone was me, with all my problems with the justice system, with the trials in progress... I can say that my arrival in their lives was chaotic.

Still, for me, it was like a rainbow after a long and heavy storm.

Every day, Uncle Ted goes to work on a magazine with Uncle Mark, and I help them with the housework. They get annoyed, saying that I don't need to do the housework, that they can hire someone for this service, and that I need to dedicate myself to school. But the truth is that I got used to it. So as soon as I finish my homework, I clean the house, cook for us, and I feel happy afterward. We have dinner together every night. It's our rule and my favorite time of the day. My uncles are a lot of fun; they're always in a good mood and deal with everything lightly, even in the most difficult situations. Hearing them talk about their problems at work is a comedy show. They make me laugh a lot. Of course, this doesn't solve all my problems, but it helps. They help me forget what I've been through and what is still ahead.

Every night during dinner, I say the prayer my father taught me, blessing our food before we eat, and we all give thanks.

"Would you hand me the knife, Nora? But slowly, so I can be sure I won't be next on your list," said uncle Mark one night. Uncle Ted pretended to be scared.

"Nora, be smart. We're the only ones left. If you kill us, who's going to sing

"True Colors" with you?"

I was silent for a few seconds as if analyzing their plea before I passed Uncle Mark the knife.

"You draw a hard bargain! Fine, today is your lucky day. I'll let you live."

Some people might find this humor absurd and dark, but we always laugh about it. It is the way we've found to deal with this matter naturally and without much suffering. This week we had the misfortune of seeing the news a few times on TV about my upcoming trial. I'm getting scared of the picture of me they chose to show on the News—I look rather insane. Uncle Mark says it's a great cover photo for a horror movie. Uncle Ted thinks I look like a junkie, with dark circles under my eyes deeper than the Hudson River. I agree with them both.

The press has constructed an almost fantastical narrative about me and the public, well... The public cannot help but be interested in what is disruptive, whatever is shocking enough. And if the public wants blood, the press will report it. That's how it works. My experience with the media shows that they want to transform everything into some sort of soap opera, something that will satisfy the appetite of the masses for cruelty. They don't care about the consequences of that freak show in the lives of the people involved. It's a dirty game, but there's nothing we can do now. Unless we no longer watch the news until the trial date. No matter how much we prepare ourselves, measuring the impact it can have on us when we're alone with our ghosts is very difficult. And what's more, the three of us made a commitment to arrive in Alabama for my trial with our heads held high, like the united family we are.

As the seemingly interminable week ends, Uncle Ted gets a call. It's the lawyer who will defend me, Stephanie O'Brien. She wants us to meet to discuss the charges before the trial, which will take place the following Monday. Uncle Ted, who previously seemed calm and secure with the trial, exchanges startled looks with Uncle Mark. The atmosphere is tense between us. Reality sets in again. We pack our bags and board the plane to Alabama from Friday to Saturday at dawn.

Arriving at Montgomery Airport, a small crowd awaits us with posters in their hands, shouting and cursing, *Justice! Jail! Monster! Slag! Daughter of Satan! Killer!* And before they build a fire right there and throw me into the flames, we manage to get out of the airport. Uncle Ted tries to protect me, but it is in vain. The inquisitors run after us. When we get a cab, I notice that part of my Alabama family is pulling the stoning symphony among the most agitated protesters—my late uncle John's wife, Elizabeth. She even bangs on the car window. With her, I recognize her children, my cousins, Eliza, Asher, and Bob. My stomach starts to turn, and right there inside the car, I grab the first plastic bag I can find and throw up.

In a second, the memories of when I lived with them on their farm are reborn more vividly than ever. When I get to the hotel room, I lock myself in the bathroom. My desire is to rip all my skin off. My breath is short, and my hands are trembling as I search every cabinet for something sharp. I want to scream and break everything. I was starting to lose my sanity, but I opened the last cabinet and saw some tiny little scissors. A sick impulse took control of me, and I cut myself. For some reason, seeing my own blood calms me down. I sit on the bathroom floor, leaning on the door as the blood drips on the green tile and my clothes. Uncle Ted knocks on the door, asking if I'm okay. Suddenly, a deep calmness goes over me, and I can convince him to leave me alone.

"I'm just taking a shower," I tell him.

It's been a long time since I stopped hurting myself. It's strange to be in this situation again. I thought I had managed to overcome these impulses, but apparently, it's as if they never went away.

I stay in the bathroom for almost two hours. Uncle Mark also knocks on the door asking for me. I replied that I was about to get in the shower and needed some time to process what had just happened. When I go under the water, I see the red water running down the drain, and I even smell my blood. I feel weak and tired. The lies about me come back to disturb me deeply. And at that moment, I realize that no matter how well accompanied I am, no matter how wonderful my uncles are to me, I will always be alone. We are always alone inside.

When I calm down, I pick up the bloody clothes from the floor and start washing them in the shower. I want to leave everything clean, without a trace. I don't want my uncles to know what I just did. I'm already such a burden to them. I don't want to add one more problem. It's for the best.

When I get out of the shower, I close my eyes, take a deep breath, cover the wounds, and put on an outfit that hides the bandages. Then, I fix my face and pretend I'm fine.

Later the same day, Ms. O'Brien, the lawyer, meets us in a room at the Hotel, so we can talk. First, she talks privately to Uncle Ted and Uncle Mark in the Hotel lobby. I can see them from where I am, but I can't hear them. Uncle Ted looks agitated—he crosses his arms, scratches his head, and walks in circles. Uncle Mark remains motionless with his intense gaze on her. Ms. O'Brien hands them some documents, and they sign everything.

Soon after, we all gather in the room where I am. Once we are seated, I ask to speak alone with the lawyer for a few minutes. They look at each other, and my uncle Ted gives his permission, saying he'll be outside if I need anything. I'm a little embarrassed to be alone with the lawyer; she expresses herself formally, and the way she looks at me makes me want to fix my posture. Though I'm nervous, I'm the one who starts talking.

"Are these forms from people you defended?"

"Some," she replies in a dry tone.

"How many of your clients tell you they are not guilty?"

"All of them."

She stares at me deeply. I feel uncomfortable and dizzy as if the ground is going to disappear. I look at those forms, and I can't stop thinking that each piece of paper is a person. Someone's fate's being sealed in those pages. I sometimes think I've been treating this subject—my accusations, the repercussions of the case, and my losses—as if they weren't real, as it was an invention, a nightmare. I can't wait to wake up and realize it's only a dream, that nothing of that horrible things happened to me…I think this is the way I found to deceive myself. I lie and pretend to keep going, to be able to look at this woman in front of me and not go crazy. But I can't always sustain the lies I tell myself, and it's precisely at those times that I have some physical implications. Sometimes Hurricane Nora messes things up in a way that makes it very difficult to measure the extent of the destruction.

I look at Ms. O'Brien and plea that I'm not guilty.

"That's really good. You should say it wasn't you."

"But I swear it wasn't me!"

"You know there are reports in which you confirm some of the accusations, don't you?"

"I was confused; it just happened. Who has the brain to answer things at a time like this?"

"I'll do my job."

"Do you believe me?"

"I'll do my job no matter what I believe, Nora."

"Of course it matters! I'm just another case for you, like these here! Right? One more name on a pile, a number on your list. I was hoping you'd be different."

"Jesus, Nora! I believe you, but that doesn't help us at all, does it? I need to prove you

didn't do what they think you did, that's all it matters, okay?"

"You don't know what it's like to hear what people say about me..."

"I know, Nora! It's horrible! That's why we need to show your humanity to them."

"My humanity. What does that mean?"

"Awaken empathy."

"Do I have to play the poor-innocent-girl card for them to believe me?"

"You need to allow yourself to talk about what you're going through, talk about what you feel."

"Do you think I have a chance?"

"My job is to try to give you one," she says, staring at me with hopeful eyes.

A while later, my uncles joined in the conversation. Ms. O'Brien reveals that the prosecutor, Kurt Smith, had contacted her a few days before to get her to drop the case, proposing a deal that would resolve everything faster, putting me in prison. She explained that prosecutor Smith is very ambitious and often makes several deals behind the scenes with very powerful people. Now, he is using my case as a springboard to gain notoriety and fund his career in politics. She said that we have to be very careful with everything we say, as Mr. Smith is influential, and his character is extremely dubious.

Uncle Ted looks dejected by what Ms. O'Brien says, and I think he wants to certify if she is indeed on our side.

"What did you say to the prosecutor when he made you the offer?"

"Don't worry. I said that I believed Nora was innocent, that she would never be able to commit such barbaric crimes."

"And what was his reaction?"

"Terrible, he's the type who doesn't know how to hear "no." He said I would regret my decision."

"Right…" said Uncle Ted nervously.

"I told him to do his job, and I would do mine. Mr. Smith, although well-connected, is not a good prosecutor. He gets angry easily."

"And is that good for us?"

"When a person doesn't know how to lose, she is easily taken by impulses that can do them harm. We can use that against him in court."

"One last question, Ms. O'Brien, does this prosecutor know the judge who will preside over Nora's case?"

"Judge Cassidy. I don't know the level of relationship between the two. Anyway, she seems to be a serious judge. I've never heard rumors of her being involved in any scamming. We're going to have to trust her. Well, I'll be off. I'll be on my phone if you need anything. We'll stay in touch. The most important thing is for you all to rest and get ready. See you Monday at the courthouse."

When Ms. O'Brien finished talking, I felt a chill down my spine. The day of the trial was approaching, and there was nothing I could do about it but wait. After the meeting, we returned to the hotel room and stayed there. The sound of the clock ticking off made us anxious. We tried to distract ourselves but to no avail. An intermittent alarm pounded in our heads— the trial, Mr. Smith, Judge Cassidy, the media, the public opinion, Ms. O'Brien, and everyone else. The impossibility of leaving that hotel without being shunned in the street haunted us. Everything, absolutely everything, seemed too much to us. We felt like prisoners, and that situation would only get worse...

On the following day, which was a Sunday, we heard a commotion outside the hotel. Later we were told that a group of people had found out where we were staying, and again, several people shouted insults at me. This time, even more angrily and inflamed than before. The protesters even broke the glass door of the Hotel, trying to break in. I started to fear for our lives, but a while later, the police arrived and dispersed the group. That evening, we saw everything on the News.

My trial had become one of the most commented topics on the internet. The three of us had fake profiles on the networks to keep track of what was happening. There was a bit of everything, different groups investigating on their own, detractors, fans, "haters," death threats, and prayer requests. The network was in an uproar. "Nora Bailey, the cancer of a generation," "Nora Bailey, the sign of the end times," "Nora Bailey, queen," "Nora Bailey, we love you." This was completely out of control. People looked like animals. And it was all very absurd.

Some wanted my head on spikes, and others tried to make me a symbol of a revolution. I attracted the attention of all sorts of freaks, fanatics, and criminals in the sewer, just waiting for an excuse to emerge. This all started to worry me even more. I couldn't stop thinking about Uncle Ted and Uncle Mark. All that exposure and hatred could fall back on them, and I wouldn't forgive myself if something happened to them.

I wish I could have an ordinary life with ordinary problems and common teenage challenges. Instead, I must carry the whole world on my back, a blind and angry world that constantly endangers the people I love. With everything happening to me, it's very difficult to lay my head on the pillow and sleep. It's like I'm always in danger. Any noise, no matter how low, makes my heart race. Tonight will for sure be another night in which I can't sleep. I've had many sleepless nights since this all started, but with the trial scheduled for the next day, it gets even more complicated. There's nothing to soothe my chest, nothing that makes me relax.

As I knew it would happen, I couldn't sleep a wink; I turned to one side, then the other, and lay on my back, my stomach, and nothing. I took sleeping pills, but nothing worked. My uncles slept heavily in the bed beside me—uncle Ted and uncle Mark looked exhausted. This whole story had worn them both out.

Taking advantage of the fact that they sleep soundly, I decide to go for a walk and get some air outside. I disguise myself well by putting on lots of coats, so they won't notice me on the street, and I walk around Montgomery. Even with the cold biting my skin, I can finally breathe. A million things go through my head, but the cruelest thing is that this might be one of my last walks as a free person. So whenever I look at something, I consider it as if it were the last time I saw it. Everything seems more beautiful to me; everything has more charm and color.

It's January, and Winter here is intense at this time of year. However, I do not let the cold air entering my lungs discourage me from walking. I am reviving myself, feeling life pulsating within me as I stroll aimlessly. I walk through unfamiliar streets, I go through scary, dark places, but nothing intimidates me. All that matters is that, at this moment, I am free.

Without realizing it, I kept going further away without direction or reason. I have no compass. I just wanted to find myself. As the minutes go by, I am already far from the hotel when I look back and realize I have no idea where I am.

All of a sudden, I realize I'm right in front of the courthouse. Without knowing how, or having decided to end up here, I feel that something has somehow pulled me to this place. So I look at the monument representing justice and say out loud, "I'm here. Now what?"

Nothing, there's no answer. Maybe justice is both blind and deaf. I look at the place, examining every detail, looking for answers to thousands of questions, but all I see is a dead end. I decide to sit there for a few moments.

My mind takes me back to my parents, my life with them, my life before all the terrible things that happened to me. I decide to say a prayer to the blind and deaf justice statute so that maybe she could see and hear me. I pray she will let me down again. I wish my parents were with me. Perhaps they are. Maybe they've been with me all along, and that's why I made it this far. Who can tell?

When I'm about to get up to go back to the Hotel, two kittens approach me, one chubby striped and the other black and white. They come softly, gaining confidence, and one even jumps on my lap. I take a cookie out of my pocket and put it out for them to eat, but they just smell it and leave it there, not interested in the treat. I spend some time with them, and while I caress them, they keep coming back to me, making me feel better. I don't know if it's all in my head, but it seems they know what's happening to me. They know something's wrong. They say animals feel these things. I want to believe they do.

I decide to return to the hotel; after all, it's late, and I worry about my uncles alone. They would be very scared if they woke up and didn't see me. I walk around for a while until I find a taxi cab.

The driver starts a conversation as soon as I get in the car. His name is George K., a big-nosed gentleman with sunken eyes and thin lips, who looks like a cartoon character with a sweet, smooth voice that sounds like a gentle grandfather. Mr. K. tells me the story of his three daughters, his struggle to raise money for the youngest one's college education, the eldest's wedding, and the middle child's summer study abroad program. Within minutes, it was as if we already knew each other for years.

At a certain point of the trip, Mr. K. looks in the rearview mirror and says in a gossipy tone, "Did you hear about tomorrow's trial? Everybody is talking about it! It's going to be over there in the courthouse, close to where I picked you up."

"Yeah."

I hide a good part of my face out of fear of being discovered and avoid speaking too much.

"I think it's absurd."

"What? What are you talking about?"

"I can't say if she's guilty or not, but these vultures don't have the slightest decency to talk about anyone these days."

"Do you think so?"

"What I know is that there are many people who take advantage of bad news to sell newspapers."

"I think so too."

"The girl is not from here, is she?"

"No."

"Tomorrow, this place will be full of journalists and people who have nothing to do with the case. The News only talks about this trial. One of the victims seems to be a large landowner in the region. His wife is always giving interviews now."

"Elizabeth is her name."

"That's right. She's the one person who had a lot to gain from this tragedy. She inherited all her husband's assets, right?"

"Yep."

"They say it's a fortune. I wouldn't even know what to do with that much money. But my life is different. I still need to work hard for my girls. You're here in this hotel, aren't you?"

"Yeah, thank you, Mr. K. Good luck to you and your daughters."

"Thank you, miss!"

When I slam the car door, Mr. K. calls me back and says with complicity:

"Good luck tomorrow, kid!"

I look at him with fear and, without reaction, I watch as he nods his head and drives away. Mr. K. knew who I was! From the beginning, he recognized me and still treated me with respect. I feel partly relieved to receive proper treatment from a stranger who could have been hostile to me. Still, I can't help but think about the risk I took. I can't tell my uncles any of this. They might have a stroke if they hear about what I did.

I walk into the room, and Uncle Ted and Uncle Mark are still asleep. I lay my head on the pillow and stare at the ceiling. I feel satisfied and even proud of myself for being so courageous. I think that despite tomorrow, my conscience is as clear and calm as a lake, and that's what makes me keep my sanity.

I'm not what the papers say; I'm not what the headlines sell. Tomorrow I won't allow myself to be ashamed of anything. I won't be afraid at all. Tomorrow I will be brought to trial, and even with an uncertain fate, even without knowing what my enemies are plotting, I will remain firm and loyal to what I am, just as my parents did all their lives. They can use justice to condemn a righteous person, but time always reveals the face of the real criminals. The truth is obtained through dedication and time, and it almost always takes time to come to the surface. But once it is out, there is no shadow or fog capable of hiding it.

Chapter Two

Day 1 - Trial

There was a gloomy and cloudy sky on Monday morning.

I was tired because I was up all night tossing and turning in bed. After a short night's sleep, I wasn't ready to tackle what awaited me. Amid the chaos, I give no thought to what Ms. O'Brien said about showing humanity to those around me. I get up and dress hastily, and we rush to court without breakfast, so we wouldn't be late.

Upon arrival, a small crowd of photographers, journalists, and onlookers gather around the front door. Some scream, *Murderer!* Some shout, *Justice!* I see people stretching and praying as I walk toward the interior of the building, feeling nothing except drowsiness, which makes me confused and hesitant. Uncles Mark and Ted lead me toward the entrance, holding my hand. I keep my head high. Upon entering, they hug me with tears in their eyes and tell me everything will be fine. I can't assimilate that this is really happening to me. I feel strangely calm. I look at the two of them with tenderness and say that they look beautiful, all suited up.

Inside, a bright white light irritates my eyes. The smell of wood and old upholstery fills the place. Everywhere I look, I see marble sculptures and paintings with faces and names I don't know—photos of old white men with erect postures. The architecture of the place is robust and imposing; it was made to last, and it seems indestructible. The furniture appears cold and sober, with a suffocating atmosphere. I walk through the halls as if through a museum where nothing can be touched. My uncles go right ahead, along with Ms. O'Brien, who leads us to the courtroom.

When we get there, I watch the prosecutor, Mr. Smith, arrive. I stare at him coldly... This is the face of the man responsible for this circus. I imagined him to be physically different, more intimidating, and with a villainous beard. Still, I see a middle-aged man with a suit too big for his short body.

He seems to have an angry temper, like a small dog that barks but does not bite.

When Judge Cassidy enters, we all stand up. She calls the jury, and they enter with their eyes lost and their faces as if they were blank sheets. I sense hollowness in each of those individuals; they don't tell me anything. They look like men and women who are there to put up a show. Perhaps. Deep down, I believe nobody there cares about me; they just want to be a source of "entertainment."

Prosecutor Smith starts talking as if every word that comes from his mouth is shiny. Still, the only thing that is really shiny is his bald head reflecting the light of the courtroom like a polished egg. I'm not too fond of anything about this gentleman, but his smug voice disgusts me. I despise people who think they're superior to others—Mr. Egghead demonstrates his arrogance by looking up and down at Ms. O'Brien and me. I desire to be able to show the middle finger and tell him to go to hell. Unfortunately, I need to behave, be the "adult" they want me to be, listen without blinking to all that insanity and say: *Yes sir, no sir.* I need to look "nice" in the eyes of the Jury. I think all of this is awful; this formalism hides the absurd hypocrisy aspect of this system. I understand why it exists, but when it goes beyond its need, it only serves the vanity of men.

"Ladies and gentlemen, my name is Kurt Smith, and I'm an assistant attorney for the state of Alabama. I represent the people in this courtroom. The Montgomery District Attorney is pleased to announce the indictment of Nora Bailey. Miss Nora is charged with three crimes. In the first of them, she is accused of killing her parents, Otto and Giovanna Bailey, by poisoning them. She is also accused of killing her uncle John Bailey with a baseball bat. Last but not least, and equally cruel, she is charged with killing her maternal grandparents, Tony and

Marie Bell, purposely causing a gas leak. We need to be aware that there was tragedy and pain wherever Nora went. The only common element in all these crimes is unequivocally one, Nora's presence. Make no mistake, ladies and gentlemen, Nora is not a child. She is a young woman who knows very well what is right and wrong. She knew exactly what she was doing. She deserves to be judged by such awareness.

When Mr. Egghead finishes speaking, Ms. O'Brien starts my defense, "Ladies and gentlemen, I'm Ms. O'Brien, defense attorney for Miss Nora Bailey. Mr. Smith will present this case to you in an extravagant, alarming, and pompous manner. But I would like to ask everyone not to forget that our laws, in addition to protecting our citizens, must also protect the accused, giving her the presumption of innocence until proven otherwise."

Mr. Egghead takes the floor again, "Ladies and gentlemen, what made us leave our homes to be here today? Some may say they came to see justice done, and I want that too. Others might say it was to better understand the horrors this young lady practiced, afraid that their children would become someone like her. I also share this fear. Still, some came this far because they still doubt they have come to be convinced that the accused is guilty. In that case, I am here to answer all their questions and ensure compliance with the law so that all our citizens feel protected... My only hope is that threats as evil as this cease to exist in our society because, contrary to what many think, justice, and God are never separated. Today we're going to tackle Nora's first crime, the murder of her parents."

Then Ms. O'Brien confidently addresses the jury, "Many people are wrongly accused of crimes, and there is nothing more terrible than putting someone behind bars for a crime they didn't commit. Contrary to what Mr. Smith says, Nora was just a girl, a child, when her parents passed. She is as much a victim as her parents, grandparents, and uncle, ladies and gentlemen."

At that moment, Mr. Egghead raises the tone of his "acting" and talks in a blatant and quite exaggerated way. It was so much that Ms. O'Brien cried, *I object!.* But Judge Cassidy lets him go on with his absurdities. At one point, Mr. Egghead approaches to affront me in a cowardly way, revealing himself to be a man not only lacking stature but also lacking virtue and a soul.

"How could you? I know what you did! You can't fool me! You are not a girl. You are a monster."

"Your Honor, I object!" Ms. O'Brien said.

And finally, Judge Cassidy receives Ms. O'Brien's objection, "Granted."

"There was an animal on the road. That's what caused the accident. How many times will I have to repeat it?" I tell Mr. Egghead.

"An animal on the road? The defendant is trying to confuse this jury. There was no animal involved in the accident, Your Honor. Several searches were carried out in the region for this animal, and nothing was found," he said mockingly.

I look at Mr. Egghead and can't believe what I'm seeing. He walks towards Judge Cassidy, and grotesquely, he lands his body next to her and speaks in a flirtatious tone as if trying to seduce her, "Of course, what I'm saying here should not be news to you, since in addition to being a very intelligent and beautiful woman, you also have a vast influence... You must have already made sure of all this, am I right?"

The ego of certain men is impressive. The confidence they have in themselves is unshakable.

Judge Cassidy takes a deep breath and, almost rolling her eyes, says firmly, "Mr. Smith, restrict yourself to commenting on just the case! My influence or anything of that nature has nothing to do with this issue."

And like a dog, Mr. Egghead returns to his seat with his tail between his legs. Ms. O'Brien looks at me with a crooked smile, demonstrating that what had just happened was good for us. At that moment, I started drawing Mr. Egghead's caricature on the paper in front of me. It's a bad caricature, I don't have much talent for drawing, but by doing that, I keep my cool through all this awfulness. I show the picture to Ms. O'Brien, and she laughs. The sketch shows an egg with a tie, an angry face, and short legs. I look at Mr. Egghead when he realizes we are making fun of him, and I see him even more determined to finish me off.

Ms. O'Brien gets up and asks Mr. Egghead, "Mr. Smith, are you a God-fearing man?"

"Yes, ma'am!"

"Do you believe the Bible?"

"Yes, ma'am!"

"Do you follow what is in the Bible?"

Mr. Egghead addresses Judge Cassidy, "Do I have to answer that, Your Honor?"

"No. Answer if you like."

Mr. Egghead replies to Ms. O'Brien, "I'm a God-fearing man, Mrs. O'Brien, so I won't excuse myself from following its commandments."

"You told this court that justice and God cannot be separated. What did you mean by that?"

"I object, your honor," Mr. Egghead says.

At this point, Judge Cassidy thinks for a few seconds, but she soon allows Ms. O'Brien to continue, "Overruled."

"I want to know, Mr. Smith, how you will conduct Nora's case. Will you follow the rules of men or God?"

Disdaining Ms. O'Brien, Mr. Egghead addresses Judge Cassidy, "Do I need to answer, Your Honor?

"No. Only if you want…"

Mr. Egghead doesn't answer Ms. O'Brien's question. He gets up, looks for the journalists among the people, and addresses them when he speaks again, "I ask you to look at this girl. Do not be deceived by her appearance, for this creature is evil incarnate."

I stop myself from laughing, but a weak, shameless laugh escapes me, causing Mr. Egghead to rage even more.

"See, Your Honor, she mocks this courtroom! And she mocks the Lord, our God!"

"I object, your honor! She mocks you, Mr. Smith!" Ms. O'Brien says.

"Order in my court!" Judge Cassidy demands it, hitting her gavel three times.

Mr. Egghead resumes his show, talking about my parents. At that moment, I low down my head and try not to think about the accident, but the images keep popping up and throbbing with my heart. I feel a tightness in my chest and everything drags me back to the day it all happened.

Mr. Egghead continues, "How would a man with his whole life ahead of him, who was extremely careful, a great scientist, with many plans for the future, put his own life and the life of his family at risk? The same I say to his wife, a loving mother, and spouse with a perfect family; how could this woman who had nothing to complain about attack her own family? Tell me! How could this perfect couple ever act like this? I say that, ladies and gentlemen, because the possibility of an accident was ruled out. Nora suggested that there was an animal on the road to the nurses who rescued her. Still, the cause of her parents' death was poisoning. Nora poisoned her own parents! That's what happened."

At that moment, I look at Ms. O'Brien with some despair and unease, and she soon realizes that everything has started to get to me. She takes my hand, looks me in the eyes, and tells me to take a deep breath, and that she was there with me. But the only thing I can feel is guilt. Guilt runs through my veins and consumes me from the inside out, and as much as I rationally repeat to myself that I had nothing to do with it, I feel like I have. I internally give myself countless justifications for what I could have done to avoid the accident, to change what happened. Even being innocent, I soon feel truly responsible for the death of my parents. I'm guilty of not having done enough; I'm guilty of not realizing that something was wrong; guilty of having survived the accident; guilty of not enjoying being their daughter while they were still here... I've been doomed since they were gone.

Mr. Egghead requests the presence of his first witnesses in the courtroom, and when I see who it is, I can hardly believe it. It's our neighbors! The neighbors my father trusted are now here to testify against me. They started by saying that our house was noisy and that I was always listening to loud music.

"What teenager doesn't listen to loud music? Is that a crime now? This is absurd!" I can't hold it.

"Aside from the loud music from the Baileys' house, how would you describe Nora as your neighbor?" Mr. Egghead asks.

Mary Fleming begins to speak. She is a gossip in our neighborhood; she knows about everyone's life and always makes up stories about people. She once said that she saw some boys smoking pot for their parents so that they wouldn't stay out late. She is an unloved woman who is always finding reasons to belittle people. And guess what she starts talking about? My appearance! Of course, this is typical of these people.

"Nora is such a pretty girl, but she always hid behind hoodies, even in the summer. Always wears black and her hair always covers her face. I've commented several times to my husband Nolan that I thought she was strange. She was never much for interacting with us."

Nolan Fleming speaks next. Nolan is a man commanded by his wife, everything she asks, he does. He is a man who lives talking about others people's possessions, and it only takes a few minutes of conversation to understand how resentful and frustrated he is.

"I hardly saw this girl. She always seemed to be hiding from us. I always talked to her father; we were friends. But what I can say about Nora is that, as rarely as we saw her, we always heard her, one way or another. We could hear her screams when she was arguing with her parents. They were always arguing."

"So you and Mr. Fleming heard Nora, as you say, *screaming,*" Mr. Egghead says.

"Yes! My wife and I had trouble sleeping when they were arguing."

"My witnesses report that they did not sleep well due to arguments from their neighbors' house, the Baileys. And that they could always hear Nora yelling at her parents. I want to ask you, Mr. and Mrs. Fleming, would you know how many days of the week this happened?"

The two look at each other, and the woman says, "When they weren't away, traveling, we could hear them arguing at least three times a week."

"The neighbors report hearing Nora yell at her parents at least three times a week. This is a lot, right?" Mr. Egghead asks. He goes on with his questioning as if he wants to forge evidence. "On the night before the Baileys' trip, did you see or hear anything different?"

"No," Mary Fleming answers. "But I saw Giovanna smoking outside her house. I found it strange because my husband and I didn't even know she smoked. It was quite late at night when this happened. I had gotten up to take my medicine."

"And later, when I got up to go to the bathroom, I noticed that only the light in Nora's room was on," Nolan Fleming adds. "I didn't understand it either because we knew they would leave early to travel. Otto even asked me to check out the house while they were gone."

"Thank you, Mr. Fleming. Is there anything more you and your wife want to say that is particular about the Baileys' house?"

Mrs. Fleming looks at the judge and the journalists and says beatifically, "'May Nora find her way. May she repent for what she has done to the innocent souls of her poor parents."

Soon after, Mr. Egghead thanks them and asks the Flemings to return to their seats. Next, he starts showing footage of the accident to the "audience" to shock everyone. I try to look away, but soon he catches my eye and invites me to see the twisted gears of our car.

"Well, a picture speaks a thousand words! Look how the car turned out."

I turn my head, and Mr. Egghead impetuously calls my attention, "Look, Nora! You must see it too. It's no use turning your face away. Guilt will accompany you for the rest of your days. Your parents are no longer here, and you are to blame!"

Taken by an enormous effervescence and inflamed like a pastor, Mr. Egghead continues, "Take one look over here, ladies and gentlemen. Nora Bailey's to blame for the tragic death of her parents, Otto and Giovanna Bailey. I won't sleep a single night until I prove this is true. I will let the world know that our children often become monsters, and these monsters must pay for their terrible deeds."

I look at all that circus in disbelief. I feel trapped in the Middle Ages, just like Joan of Arc, accused by decrepit old hypocrites in the name of the law of "God." How many women, girls like me, must not have been thrown into the fire like they were witches just because old slobbers like Mr. Egghead pointed the finger at them?

While Mr. Egghead speaks, the images of the accident scramble in my head. I don't know if out of shock, pain, or fear of reliving it all again, I'm thrown to the day my parents passed. The memories of that day are spiraling, and I can't help it. I'm transported to the day I had been trying so hard to forget.

It was a quiet Sunday morning, and they had arranged a few days off work, so we could travel.

"We missed church today, but we cannot miss our time with our God. Did you hear that, Nora?" My dad said.

He was a man of great faith, my mother and I just accompanied him. He always led prayers, and he gave thanks for everything. He was a very religious man.

My mother was a good and very passionate wife to him. I remember her talking about their first date, their first kiss, and even the day they made me—believe me, she told the smallest details, and she seemed to enjoy seeing my father blush whenever she started talking. She had always been like that, blunt, authentic, and romantic. For me, she was a mixture of Greta Garbo and Audrey Hepburn. My mother looked like a film star. In addition to her beauty, she had a strong, attractive force surrounding her. Everyone would stop to hear whatever she was saying, and she spoke easily about almost every subject.

On that terrible day, the two of them were very calm. They solved the trip's details very calmly; they left the house well-organized to go out as they always did. They put our luggage in the trunk, asked our obnoxious neighbors to take care of the house, and asked them to call us if they saw anything out of the ordinary.

My father, Otto, was a very methodical man; he couldn't leave any loose ends in anything, the car had to be in perfect condition, the weather had to be good to travel, there had to be little traffic, the timing had to be right, and he needed a good night's sleep. That's how it all turned out. Everything was according to what he wanted. So, technically it was supposed to be all right with the trip. But that's not how it happened, not everything is an exact science, and sometimes everything needs to be absolutely under control to go wrong.

The night before our trip, I wasn't feeling well, something dark seemed to be around me, and I couldn't sleep. I had to take my medicine to contain my anxiety. To be honest, I didn't want to visit my uncles; the idea of going to the countryside didn't appeal to me. Uncle John and Aunt Elizabeth's house was always a scary place for me. I never liked them very much. They represented the perfect family image, but only for those who saw them from the outside because they always revealed their monstrous side at some point. For me, they were always outdated troglodytes with an interior filled with prejudice, resentment, and hatred, with the veil of "faith" disguising it all.

But my father was very excited to be able to see his brothers. He went to bed early that night, anxious about our trip. I agreed to accompany him, and my mother had no excuses left; the two of us were almost always in agreement. She also felt bad at Uncle John's house.

On the farm, they all lived in a big house: Uncle John, his wife Elizabeth, and three children, Eliza, Asher, and Bob. The widower, Uncle Bruce, and his only child, Andrew.

The farm seemed hostile, with a heavy atmosphere. My mother and I felt that everyone started to speak ill of us as soon as we turned our backs. That's why we were always against going there. They were affectionate with greetings and looked us in the eye, but they always conspired against us at the first opportunity. They mocked and gloated when my father wasn't around, and he was the only one who didn't notice. They were all very "religious" and claimed to follow God's commandments, but whatever the Scripture seemed less beneficial to them, they did not delay in condemning and were more than eager to see anyone burn at stake.

On the morning of the trip, the sun had barely risen as we left Florida for Alabama. On the road, my dad would hum the song *Dixieland Delight*, and ask us to join him in the chorus, and at that point, it was no use continuing to be annoyed at having to visit my reactionary uncles, after all, to see my dad so happy made it all worth it. In fact, there had been quite some time since we didn't do something together. That trip was important to him; I could feel it. But not so much for me. I always understood the conditions that the work imposed on both of them, they were always traveling for work, and I got used to being alone. I was always alone.

Our relationship was complicated; that part was true. I spoke very little about myself, and my parents barely spoke to me about theirs. People who knew us might have thought that the three of us just lived under the same roof, but each had their private life and secrets. No one broke this silent contract and tried to change things. Still, I don't blame myself for that. I don't blame myself for anything. After all, the "adults" were them, not me. But this lack, this absence that I felt from my parents, never tarnished the admiration I felt for them. It never hurt my feelings; I loved them and always will.

At that moment, Ms. O'Brien calls my attention, asking if I'm okay and if I can continue... I say *yes*, though I was emerged in my memories.

Mr. Egghead creates a stir in the courtroom by wielding the result of his skill in hiss:

"Your Honor, I ask that everyone who has ears to listen and those who have eyes to see, here in my hand is the toxicological report of the technical expertise made on the bodies of Mr. and Mrs. Bailey. This is an important phase of the investigation that brought us here, so I would like your attention to the details in this file because here is proof that Nora's parents did not die in the accident but were poisoned."

Tension grips the courtroom, and several eyes are on me. I listened attentively to the reading of the Report, which says that they had been poisoned. Even though my lawyer already knew about this result and had communicated it to me, hearing that being said aloud to everyone made me shudder. I could never understand it all. If it's true that they were poisoned, how did that happen? Who had done it? Why? And even if someone did it, I can't puzzle together how... It doesn't make any sense to me. If something had happened, I would have noticed the difference. I would have seen if they had taken something, but I didn't notice anything. They acted *normal*. They didn't give any sign that something was up. They were as they always were. I couldn't understand.

At this moment, Mr. Egghead, with a triumphant air, invites me for an interrogation:

"Your Honor, I call Ms. Nora Bailey to the stand."

Ms. O'Brien raises immediately.

"I object! My client has the right to confidentiality."

"I'm not going to ask about what happened since you're her lawyer. I'm going to ask about what happened before." Mr. Egghead says calmly.

"I object! Your Honor, we can see how this girl is shaken by facing this trial. We can't lose sight of the fact that Nora is only sixteen years old. This is all very difficult for her, especially after enduring many family losses. It is unreasonable to make her go through this violence again."

"Overruled. Ms. O'Brien, what is or is not reasonable is not within my power. Mr. Smith, please direct the defendant to the oath and proceed with the questions, but be reasonable," Judge Cassidy says.

What's going on? I can't believe that the judge is mocking my attorney's speech that way. Egghead has a smile off his face, and the judge herself now legitimizes his attitude. I don't understand the law, but if the judge, who should be impartial, is acting like this, what should I expect? What will become of me? Wouldn't it be better to condemn me to death sooner? I feel as if I am in a nest of vipers.

"Let's go, Nora! Come take the oath in the eyes of God." Mr. Egghead says in a soft, peaceful voice.

I keep thinking... What must God think of all this? This is a circus, a freak show! God's eyes may be everywhere, but they are certainly not here. There is nothing good here. There is only evil. I think God took his eyes off me long ago; otherwise, I wouldn't even be here.

Still, I take a deep breath and try to make my way to the pulpit. I stand up slowly and feel my legs trembling. I realize that Mr. Egghead looks like he thinks it's a pretense and triangulates with a few presents with a mischievous smile on his face. I look where I need to go and feel dizzy. Mr. Egghead is amused and begins to say aloud that it is only now, when I am about to be questioned, that the uneasiness arises, "She's deceiving!"

He yells while laughing at me.

I feel like I am nothing like an abomination, a beast, a loathsome, contagious creature. And it is precisely in these moments that I question the idea of evolution in human beings. Did the Middle Ages really cease to exist? Every day I am surprised to find more specimens of that period wandering through today. There is not even a minute of peace when walking to the gallows. I look at Judge Cassidy and warn her of my possible sudden illness.

"Sorry, I think I'm going to faint."

"Oh! You're going to faint, yes. Do you want me to help you? I help you, come!" Mr. Egghead says mockingly, with an agitated and hurried voice.

At that moment, Mr. Egghead hints at touching my arms, and a deep hatred takes hold of me. I feel my entire body shaking with rage, my eyes widening, my fists clenching, and my heart beating fast as if it was about to explode. I regain my strength and want to break his teeth, but I stop to a certain extent and just scream.

"NO! Stay away from me! Don't lay your hand on me! You're disgusting, Egghead!"

When I realized what I'd said, it was too late. I shouted loud and clear for everyone in the courtroom to hear, "Egghead." Immediately, some present laugh copiously because, after all, Mr. Smth's head reflected the room's bright light, accentuating the oval shape of his head. Everybody was thinking, and I just said it out loud. In fact, I shouted. When I look at Mr. Smith, he's red as a tomato. It looks like flames of fire are coming out of his nostrils, and I enjoy myself. I even manage a small smile of satisfaction. And it is in this small revenge that I find the strength to reach the pulpit.

They put the bible in front of me, and I feel that what they are doing is wrong. It shouldn't be like this; they shouldn't play with what is sacred. My father taught me the Bible very well. However, they distort the Scripture, corrupt it, defile it and use it in their favor for their gain, money, and power. And on the pretense of doing justice, on the cornerstone of guilt, they imprison, stone, and condemn innocent people in the name of God. This can't be right!

I reach out and begin my oath.

"Do you solemnly swear to tell the truth, the whole truth, and nothing but the truth? So help you God?"

"I do."

As I do my oath, I miss my father enormously. I feel closer to him as I speak; I hear his intonation, the melody of the words when he said our prayers. My chest tightens, and I am again drawn to the trip's images, and my brain starts questioning what actually happened that day.

I remember the journey was very long, and the road never seemed to end. My dad kept playing his favorite songs over and over again. My mother was tense over something, but I couldn't distinguish it. I thought it could be because we were getting closer, which was weird for me too. But is that why, after all? Did she know about the poison? No, no! That's not possible. If that were it, she would have freaked out. I knew my mother well; we were very similar...

I took a nap when we were only a few hours from our destination. My eyes were closing, and the road seemed increasingly monotonous as it became emptier. Tiredness began to weigh heavily on everyone. My mother occasionally stretched out; my father looked like a rock, he barely moved or spoke, but his weariness was also visible.

Gradually my thoughts were shuffling somewhere between Kingston and Greenville, Alabama. Between one turn and another, I would move, say something meaningless and go back to sleep. I remember that a fine drizzle started to fall at some point, and my sleep started to get heavier. The last thing I noticed was the sunset and nightfall. I remember the smell of the wet green field, the feeling of warmth of being like in a womb, protected from the rain and the dangers of the outer world. Finally, I remember my mother's eyes on me—they were my refuge.

I was in and out of sleep, and everything felt calm and peaceful somewhere between Kingston and Greenville. Somewhere. Nowhere. Between Kingston and Greenville. It felt like I was nowhere to be found. And I was also neither asleep nor awake. Somewhere between Kingston and Greenville, somewhere between my inner self and the real world, with the sound of the gentle rain on the road. The noise of the car's engine. My mom and dad were with me, as if we were all sleeping together, in the same room, like when I was a kid.

A state of dream.

These were the moments before the whole dream ended. I felt fulfilled, united with them, as if an invisible bond had brought us together again and everything absent before no longer existed. They were there with me intimately and profoundly.

Then everything happened very fast and at the same time. The noise of wheels burning the asphalt, the smell of ashes, my mother screaming, and everything spinning: Our bodies, our things, suitcases, bags... Everything mixing up, heads, arms, legs... My last words were *mom*. The car overturned brutally. It was happening; I was there. My mother yelled something I didn't understand. She saw an animal on the road, and she shouted,

"Look out, a moose!"

This last part is not clear to me. Did my mother say that, or was it a dream? I don't know. I may have imagined it in my half-sleep mode. The density of time had changed at that moment. It was as if we had jumped into an abyss and plunged deep into the cold, dark water. I had the distinct sensation of my mother's hair on my face, of the car window shattering, of the car spinning and going deeper and deeper, as if we were diving deep into a swimming pool and feeling the water pressure in our ears. Only in this case, there wasn't any water.

I woke up in the hospital, alone. My vision was blurred, and I was very confused. I didn't know what had happened. Someone then put a bright white light in my eyes and said, "She's fine, she's fine."

I couldn't quite see what was happening, but I noticed three people in the room.

My clothes were bloody, but I couldn't see any bad injuries. Everything was hazy and disjointed...

"My glasses... Does anyone know...?" I mumbled a few words, but they asked me to close my eyes and rest.

"A moose! There was a moose on the road," I mumbled these words, closing my eyes.

I remembered my mother screaming, the diving, the smell of gasoline, the wet road, and the feeling of the windows cutting my skin. I opened my eyes again in the hospital, and with a blurred vision, I saw the horns of a large animal beside me. It frightened me greatly, and I froze.

"Did it come for me?" I whispered to the nurse, but she didn't answer me.

I tried to scream, but my voice wouldn't come out! And this time, I saw it clearly; there was a huge moose beside my bed. It looked at me and sniffled next to my face.

"Help! Help..."

I kept asking for help, but no one could hear me. I started to sob. The moose continued to stare at me, and I could feel it was about to touch me.

"Someone please help me! Get it out of here!" I kept shouting.

But my voice seemed stuck in my head. The words echoed inside me, finding no way out. The moose sniffed in my face, and I felt like this would be my end. I saw a shadow around that big animal, and my body remained motionless. I couldn't move or speak; I felt trapped within my body and couldn't find the key to get out. I wanted to hide, and I tried closing my eyes, but I felt the animal was still there.

The nurse approached me and put her hand on my chest, telling me to calm down. When I opened my eyes, I didn't see the creature anymore. "It was just a nightmare, my girl. It's all right! Everything's gonna be okay."

"Who were the other two people who were here in the room? My father, my mother?" I tried to make sense of it all.

"No, it was just me and Dr. Northon. We were here with you," she replied.

"But I saw it, I saw it! There was someone else here. I know there was."

My chest felt tight, as if I'd been crying for hours. The nurse tried to calm me down, "You're still confused, you woke up very scared, and we gave you a tranquilizer. It's normal to feel like this. You've been through a terrible trauma."

But that made me even more worried. I wanted to know where my parents were. "Where are they?"

"Don't worry about it now. We're taking care of everything. I will let you know as soon as I have any information about your parents. What you need now is rest. Are you feeling any pain?"

"On my arm."

"From a scale of zero to ten, how bad is your pain?"

"Ten"

"All right, I'll prepare a little medicine to help with the pain in your arm. I'll bring it to you soon."

I knew she wouldn't tell me about my parents, so I lied about the pain. I wanted to be alone and look for my family in the hospital. I got out of bed despite the ache I felt in my body. I had small cuts, but nothing that prevented me from walking. I couldn't see well without my glasses, but I found the hospital ward. I kept walking, looking for my parents, investigating the rooms where other patients were. I walked all the way down the hall but couldn't find them. I started to worry and ran to the hospital's main lobby. I tried to hide from the nurse there, but she soon noticed me. I kept running away from her and asking for my parents.

"Dad? Dad? Where are you, dad? Mom? Mom, where are you?"

When I arrived at the door of the ICU, I looked through the glass. What I saw made me shudder and shiver from head to toe, and I collapsed. It was the moose. It was there, staring at me once more. It looked at me deeply as if it could see through me. It was like it had something to say to me, but it didn't know how.

Sometime later, I woke up again in my hospital bed. I wasn't sure if it had all been a dream or if it had been real. The lights were off, and the silence and atmosphere of the hospital at night made me shiver again. I felt so alone and terrified at that moment that I started questioning my sanity. A series of things went through my head, *Was the accident my fault? I didn't want to go. I knew we couldn't have gone. I was sensing something. I knew something bad was going to happen. How did I let this go on? Why didn't I follow my intuition?*

I started calling for my parents from the hospital bed, "Dad, where are you? Mom, I'm afraid. Please don't leave me alone! Where are you? Why haven't you come here to see if I'm okay?"

Then I started mixing things up, saying, "Aren't you back from work yet? I already did my homework, can I show you? It's here with me."

I paced in my room in the dark. Sometimes, I talked to my parents, imagining they were there. Other times, I spoke to myself, remembering things from our past, upsetting memories, but they still made me feel better because it was as if my parents were there with me.

The nurse came in and turned on the light, "Nora, what happened? What were you doing?" She asked.

"I wasn't doing anything."

At that moment, she put something down on her clipboard. I looked at her and felt like she had a familiar face. Her face resembled my mother's, and she cared for me as my mother would.

"Come, go back to your bed. Is your pain better?"

"I don't feel any pain."

"The medicine must have started to work. I will call Dr. Northon to talk to you, okay?"

"No, don't leave me here alone."

"I'll be right back. There's no reason for you to worry, okay?"

"Alright, mom."

"Nora, I'm not your mother. I'm the nurse, Abigail, remember?"

"Have I left this room today?"

"You haven't. You need rest. But I promise that you'll be better soon."

"Do you think it was my fault?"

"Of course not, Nora! Don't think about these things now. Everything will work out, don't worry. Dr. Northon will come to talk to you."

After that, I fell asleep waiting for the Doctor. I don't know if he ever showed up. Maybe he gave up talking to me because he wanted to let me rest.

Those hours in the hospital felt like days. Everything had been very difficult and strange. I wasn't sure what had happened, if my parents were okay, if they were in that hospital with me, in the ward, the ICU… or if anyone from our family was coming to get us. My head was chaotic and confused; I still didn't understand how what I had experienced earlier, walking through the hospital halls, running away from the nurse, seeing the creature… It could not have been real.

I woke up the next day with the sunlight streaming through the blinds. I felt better and calmer, but I immediately remembered everything, and a sadness pressed into my chest. It would be easier if it were all just a dream, an invention, or a delusion, but it was real life, and I once again faced it alone.

The doctor entered my room and approached me. I strained to see the name written on his lab coat. It was Dr. Northon, the person the nurse, Abigail, had told me about.

"Good morning, Nora! How was your night?"

"I think it was okay. I don't remember it well."

"I am Dr. Northon. I was the one who welcomed you here."

"And my parents, how are they?"

"You need to be strong, okay? Your family is here. I'll authorize their entry to come to stay with you. Sounds good?"

"But where is my father? Where is my mother?"

"They didn't make it. We still don't quite understand what happened. They died before the accident, not because of it. So the bodies were sent to forensics specialists, and as soon as we have some position, we will inform your family."

And that's how I received the news that I had become an orphan. I stood still, catatonic, not knowing what to do or where to go. I was completely adrift.

"Nora, are you okay?" Ms.O'brien asks.

For a moment, I had forgotten I was in the courtroom. I respond by nodding my head, and Ms. O'Brien returns to her seat. Then Mr. Egghead begins the interrogation.

"Your Honor, I will conduct some questions now and ask you to request silence so that nothing that is said is lost or contradicted."

"Silence! Silence in the courtroom. Come on, Mr. Smith, you may start," Judge Cassidy says.

Then Mr. Egghead restarts, "I ask for the undivided attention of those present! What will be asked here is extremely important for understanding this case and for resolving all the crimes committed. Are you ready, Nora?"

I answer bluntly, "I don't know the law you follow, nor how you will manipulate this case, so no, I'm not ready."

"Worse for you, isn't it?" He teases.

"This law exists only in your imagination," I answer.

I start to say what I think and feel without considering the effects on the jury or Judge Cassidy. But Mr. Egghead gets angry and starts trying to intimidate me.

"You will soon feel the weight and effect of this law!"

Courage loses up tongue, "You're only here for the repercussion of the case, for the fame! You should be ashamed!"

At that moment, Mr. Egghead looks like he wants to jump into a rage fit. He aggressively approaches me and speaks, almost shouting, "You will embitter the rest of your days in jail, insolent girl! I will put you there and ask them to throw the key away."

"I object, your Honor. He's intimidating my client," Ms. O'Brien intervenes.

I tell Ms. O'Brien not to worry because I can handle it. But she and Mr. Egghead begin to face each other, and Judge Cassidy bangs her gavel, appealing for order, and addresses me with great seriousness and decorum, "Nora, this is the house of justice and deserves to be respected as such. The law, as well as justice, exists and does not choose or differentiate. It judges everyone, and we are all subject to it. You are still very young, I can understand your impulsiveness to a certain extent, but this court does not run away and does not exempt itself from fulfilling its duties and responsibilities in the search for the truth. You will be judged as required by law, and nothing will alienate these negotiations."

I lower my head and watch Mr. Egghead's pedantic attitude toward Judge Cassidy, "Thank you, Your Honor! There is transparency in this courtroom! As everyone can see, the defendant admits and claims not to know the law and is still innocent." Then he addresses me with a know-it-all smirk, "Nora, these are two things that cannot coexist. Who are you trying to deceive?"

Judge Cassidy impatiently says, "Come on, Mr. Smith, get to your point without further ado. Otherwise, I will suspend your questions and release the defendant."

"Very well, your honor."

He straightens his tie, stretches his shirt under his suit, runs his hand over his bald head, and like a pastor taken by the Holy Spirit, he approaches me, "Nora, did you know that your parents were environmental toxicologists and that they were doing scientific research in the Everglades National Park?"

"Yes," I answer.

"Is it true that your parents traveled a lot to the detriment of work?"

"Yes."

"And how did you feel?"

"Alone, but I always understood their reasons."

"So, was it common for you to be left alone?"

"Yes, except when Mrs. Nancy, who worked in our house, was there."

"Whose presence was restricted only to the shift of her work in the house, correct?"

"Yes."

"And what did you do when you were alone, Nora?"

Ms. O'Brien interrupts Mr. Egghead, "I object. How does that have anything to do with the case, Your Honor?"

"Sustained, get to the point, Mr. Smith," Judge Cassidy says.

Mr. Smith resumes his reasoning with an air of superiority, "Fine, is it true that you spent many hours alone, Nora?"

"Yes, I just told you."

"And is it true that you had unrestricted access to your parents' work materials?"

"Yes, but I barely entered their room, and I never went through their things."

"But did you ever move them?"

"Out of curiosity, maybe, I messed it up."

"Yes, you moved their things! We found your fingerprints in your parents' work materials."

"I may have gotten it for them at some point."

"Did you know, Nora, that your father and mother manipulated poisonous plants in their work?"

"Yes, they told me not to touch some of their things because it was dangerous."

"But still you decided to disobey your parents?"

"I did not disobey them."

"Is it true that you knew about the manchineel tree?"

"Yes, my parents talked a lot about it."

"So I can assume that you also knew the manchineel is commonly known as the apple of death."

"Yes, so?"

"Nora, have you ever touched your parents' materials that contained the name of this tree or plant on the label?"

"No. Not that I remember!"

"Your Honor, here is the expert report that shows Nora's fingerprints in the pot that contained this poisonous plant."

Mr. Smith delivers the report to the Judge.

"But I didn't move it! I didn't! They may have used the same pot from another plant," I hurriedly told Mr. Egghead.

"Nora, your father was a very meticulous man, wasn't he?"

"Yes, he was, but I…"

Mr. Egghead interrupts me to talk to Judge Cassidy while handing her other files.

"It is part of the protocol that these pots are never reused. This is a rule for everyone who works in this profession. Here it is…"

Judge Cassidy examines the file she has just received with her glasses. Meanwhile, Mr. Egghead continues to address me with a teasing tone, "You don't want us to believe that your father, a responsible man, an excellent professional, would have committed such inattention, do you, Nora?"

"My father was a very careful man, but something must have happened. I don't know how to explain it," I said.

"You don't know what, Nora? Don't you know if you came into contact with the poison in one of those pots and manipulated it?"

"I don't know…"

Mr. Egghead interrupts me again, "Your honor, the defendant claims not to know whether she manipulated the pot containing a poisonous drug, which led to her parents' death. Let this be in the record."

"That is not what I said! I…"

Interrupting me again, Mr. Egghead starts talking about my mother, "Nora, calm down, let's continue. Is it true that your mother, Giovanna Bailey, despite going out in the field with your father, was left with the most bureaucratic part of the job?"

"Yes, I mean… My mother also did everything else. She was very good, so she ended up doing the practical part also, like taking care of most of the bureaucracy, delivering reports and cataloging the findings."

"Did you consider her a brilliant scientist?"

"Yes, my mother was the best!"

"Your honor, a respected scientist, a very intelligent woman, would she let a child, her child, get close to something she knew and considered so dangerous? I do not think so!"

Mr. Egghead is now more sadistic than ever. It's almost like he's drooling. His gaze carries something sickly, like a vulture on flesh. And I understand his game, I'm taken by it, and I don't even claim anything anymore; I don't care about myself anymore. I've been attacked in such cruel ways that being used as a piece, a pawn in a game of chess in such a vile way, doesn't surprise me or hurt me as I thought it would. I am shattered, and my disbelief in human kindness crystallizes. Now I always expect the worst; it became my natural reflex.

Judge Cassidy takes the floor and asks for a two-hour recession. By now, everyone is quite weary. Ms. O'Brien wants to use this time to discuss possible paths for me to take, but I refuse. I want to be alone; I need space to breathe.

I sit on a bench outside, away from the media's hustle and the curious stares, and I watch people passing by. I imagine for a moment the life they are living, who they are, what they do... I try to guess everything about them by their clothes and jewelry as if I am trying to unpuzzle a mystery. I look at these people, and I imagine I become them... I imagine I have another name, another life, another story. I imagine myself with a less tragic life, with less suffering, with "normal" problems—an ordinary life. And in this game, as time passes, I get distracted, and without realizing it, a man sits next to me. He has a husky and soft voice, and he catches my attention. He is a rather thin gentleman in his early sixties, with a creased, weathered face, dressed in a faded brown coat. He looks at me for a few moments, I look at him, and as someone who asks, not wanting to get in the way, he starts the conversation with me:

"Hey!"

"Hey," I answer.

"What are you doing here, girl?" He asks with a worried air.

"I am waiting," I answer with a tired and hopeless smile.

"What are you waiting for?" He asks as he looks up.

"The trial," I answer.

And then he bursts out laughing as if I had said a joke, and a very good one.

"Sorry. I'm just an old man with a great sense of humor. But I get it, girl, I get it! And aren't we all waiting for the final trial, the judgment day? You see, even I, a tired and inconsequential old man, have been waiting for it..."

"What is your name?"

"Why does my name matter, child? I'm just an old man! What about yours? What's your name?"

"Why doesn't your name matter, and mine does?"

"Great question! You're a pretty smart girl, I can tell. Your name matters, my child, because you are the future."

"The future? How so?"

"Your name matters because you are young! Young people are the most important people."

"Why? Nothing ever changes, young or old. The world remains the same," I answer, feeling hurt by my reality.

"Oh, my child! What a sad sight. The world is in motion, and it's in construction and deconstruction, perpetuum mobility. You carry great suffering, don't you?"

The old man intrigues me. He uses words but never holds to their literal meaning. He always seems to be saying more than he says when he speaks. And he seems to see me more than I'd like to show. I try to remain silent to avoid talking about myself, but he continues, "Did you know that suffering can be a great blessing and that when it comes early, it transforms the sufferer in such a way as to make them important to the world?"

Now I'm the one who laughs, but my laugh is nervous and full of barbs.

"I'm not important. I was just born with a fate doomed to sadness," I answer him, showing how much I'm hurt.

He takes a deep breath and answers me with kindness, "No! Please don't do it, don't feed the shadows, my poor girl. The more we feed the pitch, the bigger it becomes. And you will be a beacon."

"A beacon?" I ask without understanding

"You are young! Young people will be lighting up the way."

"Again you say young people are important for the world and the future. I'm not like that, okay? With me, things always end before they are built."

"Don't worry. It is like that with everyone."

"Everyone who?"

"The great brilliant minds suffer a lot. They see the future but live in the present, having to respond to outdated systems. This causes a lot of suffering, my child."

"I don't think I understand yet."

"But you will understand. It is a matter of time. As for suffering, this old man here has something to tell you…"

"Are you going to say that you have the magic formula for not suffering and want to sell me? Is that it?"

"No, that's not it. Suffering is inherent in life! But get this: When you hear a joke from someone and laugh at it, let's say that it fulfilled its role: to make them laugh. But if you are told the same joke over and over, it will lose its effect. You won't laugh about it anymore, will you?"

"Yes, it will lose its punch!" I answer.

"If that's how it is with jokes, why cry over the same problems, my girl? Don't feed the pain, don't let the pain grow in you and obscure the light you'll use to enlighten us…"

We stood there for a few minutes in silence.

"You're a very hopeful man, aren't you?" I ask him.

"It's the only thing I have. I don't own anything anymore, my girl. Hope is all that's left."

We fell silent again. The nameless old man straightens up, closes his coat and his eyes, but not to sleep. I look at him, and he seems to be meditating. He is a spiritual man, and it is pleasant to be in his company. I'm starting to think about what it means to be a spiritual person, and for me, maybe it's someone who takes responsibility for their mistakes for having made them. I think this gentleman is someone like that.

"Girl…" He calls me again. "Don't I know you from somewhere?"

I was afraid that moment would come. He must have seen me on the news and recognized me. If that's it, he wouldn't have so much hope in me. "You must have seen me on TV," I say, disappointed.

"Oh! No! No… I haven't watched TV in a long, long time."

I feel relieved. It's great to talk to someone who doesn't have a prejudgment about me. Someone that can look and talk to me and perhaps understand who I really am.

"Then I don't know how you know me."

"It must just be my impression, my girl. People felt it with them too. There are several reports."

"Who are you talking about?"

"The big ones!"

"I'm sorry, sir, but you are very weird!"

The Nameless Old Man smiles, agreeing with me.

"That sounds like music to my ears. Fitting into a cookie-cutter sick world and not being a "weirdo" is the real problem.

I smile in agreement, and he smiles back. I feel so comfortable in the presence of this gentleman. It's as if he was responsible for a break in the war. He brings me peace.

"I agree with you, *Mr. nameless*. I'm weird too."

He laughs again.

"*Mr. Nameless*, I loved that, my child. I loved it!"

"*Mr. Nameless*, who has hope in the young generation. What if I'm a criminal?"

"The young person is only the reflection of all people who are criminals."

"You always have something to say, don't you?"

"That's not a good sign, my girl. I wish I could have a mind as fruitful as yours and learn as you learn. But this old carcass talks a lot and doesn't always know why."

"I like to hear you speak."

"Listening is good. Listening is always better than talking."

The old man is quiet for a few moments, but then he speaks again,

"So you mean all that fuss outside is because of you?"

"Can you believe it? They made a spectacle out of my life."

"Hyenas! They mess with our heads."

The old man gets up, looks to the right, kneels to the left, and asks me to open my hands. He gives me a handful of strawberry candies.

"To sweeten things a little, my child. I have to go! Sorry to disturb you. I'm a lonely old man who sometimes stops by to talk to the damned. But you know, you're not one of them. You are a beacon! I feel it. You will be alright."

My eyes fill with tears. I don't want him to leave! The care I needed from those closest to me came from a stranger. It was like finding a spring after a long walk in the desert. Not everything is pitch dark, and yes, there is hope.

A few minutes later, Ms. O'Brien takes me by the arm. She urgently drags me to the courthouse, "Nora, where have you been? I've been looking for you for almost an hour. We're late. This is terrible for you!"

"But I was here the whole time. I haven't left. I didn't even go to the bathroom."

"*Here*, where no one can find you, right? Judge Cassidy may misunderstand it. This inattention may work against you."

"Whatever!" I answer.

"No, Nora! Look at me! I'm doing everything I can to prove your innocence, but you must cooperate. I won't be able to help you if you don't care about the consequences of your actions, okay?"

"Ms. O'Brien, wait! I'm willing. I understand your frustration at not having found me, but I was here the whole time, talking to a gentleman…"

Ms. O'Brien stops pacing and holds me to give me more lectures before we go inside.

"Talking to whom, Nora? Always presume someone tried to gather information about the case to use against me."

"A gentleman sat next to me, but don't worry, I didn't say anything I couldn't say," I answer.

"What was his name, Nora?"

"Mr. Nameless."

"What?"

"He didn't have a name or didn't want to say it."

"Nora, you can't talk to strangers at a time like this. Can't you see the risk you took? The whole town is itchy about this case. They're all talking about you. You need to be more careful!"

"I told you we didn't talk about the case!" I answer.

"Fine, Are you ready?"

"No, but we need to go anyway, don't we?"

She looks at me seriously, takes a deep breath, and opens the courtroom door. As soon as we enter, we see Mr. Egghead talking to another prosecutor. When he sees us, he lets out a Machiavellian smile while gloatingly looking at his watch, as if he is trying to make us understand that he feels at an advantage with the time slip. Before I can even justify myself, Judge Cassidy gets up and shouts in a loud and clear voice, "You should have introduced yourself forty-five minutes ago!"

I remain silent, embarrassed. When I try to speak, she interrupts me again, "Forty-five minutes ago…"

When she repeats the same sentence, I take a deep breath, lift my head, look into her eyes, and firmly say, "I understand you don't believe me! But I was right here next to you the whole time. I may be late, but the fact is, I'm here."

She looks at me, takes a deep breath, and says impatiently, "Fine! Let's continue the interrogation! Mr. Smith?"

"Yes, Your Honor."

"Please continue!"

"Well then! Nora, please come to the microphone."

Mr. Egghead catches the attention of the jury, which begins to return to the trial,

"Ladies and gentlemen, welcome once again! Let's continue the interrogation. Miss Nora Bailey, is it true that you take prescription drugs?"

"Yes."

"And for how long?"

"Since I was 12 years old."

"Four years, correct?"

"Yes."

"On the day of the trip with your parents, did you take your medicine?"

"No, I ran out of meds that same day."

"You ran out?" he asks, sarcastically.

"Yes," I answer.

So, could you tell us why your medicine box was found sealed in your bathroom trash?"

"No, I can't say."

"So, could you tell me where you threw your empty medicine box?"

"I don't remember very well. But I must have thrown it in the trash," I answer.

Mr. Egghead walks to the courthouse door, takes a trash can and puts it in the center for everyone to see.

"Ladies and gentlemen, think with me for a moment. Suppose that the center of this courtroom is Nora's room, and the rest of the house is outside. So this trash can here in front of me is the trash can in her room. If this bin's here, and there's another bin far away, across the street, which bin would you rather throw this paper ball into?"

At that moment, Mr. Egghead holds up a crumpled paper, and I feel self-conscious about his prosecution material. A child would do better. Is he trying to condemn me because I used the garbage outside my house? This is pathetic!

"I object! Mr. Smith continues to bring irrelevant evidence to the case." Ms. O'Brien says impatiently.

"Calm down, Ms. O'Brien! I will get to the heart of the matter," He answers.

"Denied. Continue, Mr. Smith!" Judge Cassidy says.

"The fact, ladies and gentlemen, is that no empty medicine box was found in any other garbage in the house. However, we found boxes of expired medicine for Nora's illness in several places in the house. The boxes there were not even opened! So I conclude Nora was without medication for a long time and under the influence of strong emotional feelings on the day of the trip with her parents."

"I wasn't the only one who took prescription medicine at home, Mr. Smith. My mother also used prescription drugs," I answer.

Ms. O'Brien and I started to get annoyed by Mr. Egghead, but his poor logic gave us positive results.

"Of course, we know that your mother also took prescription medication, but if she was throwing away her medication, why would she throw it in the wastebasket in your room? Your Honor, I truly believe that Nora killed her parents. She was experiencing strong emotions due to the lack of her medicine. As her neighbors reported, she was hurt by the constant friction between her and her parents. Moved by anger from her abandonment feelings, she remembered the poisonous substance at her home and prepared to act the night before the trip. She planned everything meticulously, went to her parents' office, picked up the poisonous substance, took it with her on the trip, and waited for the best moment to pour it into their drinks. Nora is an unstable person, Your Honor. She has a sick mind. That night, the only light on at the Baileys came from Nora's room. I believe it was at this time that she took advantage of the fact her parents were asleep to execute her plan. At around 4:00 PM, the Baileys' car was seen at the Nugfries Cafeteria. We have security footage to prove they were there. I believe it is at this moment, in this cafeteria, in a moment of distraction, that Nora found an opportunity and poisoned her parents' drinks. Afterward, she traveled with them as if nothing had happened until the moment of the accident when Mr. Otto Bailey felt sick and passed out while still driving. Another clue was Nora's statement regarding when she called the rescuers. She reported to the nurses that she called them at around 6:50 PM, but the accident didn't happen until 7:20 PM, as witnesses say.

I don't control myself and say loudly, "I said an approximate time. I didn't know for sure what time it was. I was stunned by what had just happened. I didn't get to call the rescuers. I already woke up in the hospital! When they asked me if I was the one who had called the rescuers, I said something, thinking they had asked what time the accident had happened, but I didn't call, I didn't!"

At that moment, Mr. Egghead turns to me and says sarcastically: "You didn't you call?! Did you say anything? So the defendant either lied to us or lied to the nurses at the hospital. Ladies and gentlemen, I ask you, why would Nora lie? No further questions."

Mr. Egghead sits down, and Ms. O'Brien gets up. "Your Honor, I would like to ask my client a few questions and clarify what was brought into questioning by Mr. Smith."

"Certainly," The judge says.

Then Ms. O'Brien approaches me, "Did you and your mother take the same medicines, Nora?"

"No, I mean… Not all of them! We took the same depression meds, but she took more…"

"These other medications, different from yours, that your mother took were not for the treatment of depression, correct, Nora?"

"Correct. Although she also took them for depression, like me."

"Right! Your Honor, if I may…"

At that moment, Ms. O'Brien opens her purse and takes out the boxes of medicine my mother used to take. She shows Mr. Egghead and then gives them to Judge Cassidy.

"Your Honor, these were the meds found at Nora's house and claimed by Mr. Smith as hers. But actually, these drugs were all from her mother, Giovanna Bailey. If you open these medications and read the package, you will understand that they are used for treating psychoses and mood stabilizers. Nora's mother, Your Honor, was diagnosed with Psychotic Depression, which is different from Nora's diagnosis."

Ms. O'Brien delivers the report from our psychiatrist to Judge Cassidy, who differentiates my illness from my mother's.

"Here in this Report, made by Dr. Anna Foley, doctor for Nora and Giovanna Bailey, you will find the report made by the psychiatrist regarding the differences between Nora's diagnosis and her mother's. And now I would like to ask some questions directed to Mr. Smith." She turns to Mr. Egghead. "Mr. Smith, did you even request a forensic examination for

Nora to identify the absence of drugs in her system, which corroborates her conclusions?"

"No, I didn't think it was necessary. After all, the medicine box was found in the trash in Nora's room. It can therefore be assumed that this medicine was hers."

"I see, so you stated that Nora murdered her own parents based on presumptions."

At that moment, Ms. O'Brien invites Mr. Egghead to go in front of the dumpster he had placed in the center of the courthouse.

"Mr. Smith, you were the one who put this bin here, right?! So let's say this trash can is yours. If I throw this candy wrapper in here, can I say with certainty that it was you who ate the candy? No, right? You also did not inform the Judge that there was not in the technical expert report that the body of Ms. Giovanna, Nora's mother, did not show the components of the medications she should have been taking. She was the one not taking the medication, not her daughter, as you are trying to prove. Mr. Smith, you cannot come to this courtroom and point the finger at this girl with fanciful inferences without bringing facts or concrete evidence proving Nora is guilty. Is your purpose here arresting innocent people, Mr. Smith? Do you want to conduct an unfair trial with speculations and convictions? It shouldn't be like that, right?"

When Ms. O'Brien finishes, I notice she is shaking, her voice breaking, and she is almost crying.

"This show of yours proves nothing!" Mr. Egghead says. "My convictions and my values will point to the truth and reveal your client's shameful actions. The people outside are crying out for justice! Everyone wants to see Nora in jail."

Mr. Egghead comes to me in a rage and threatens me in the name of God in a low tone of voice, which only I can hear, "You may even think that you will be able to escape the eyes of men, but you will never escape in the eyes of God! You are still accused and will respond to all charges during these investigations. You may even get away with one, but you will never escape all of them."

"I object, your Honor! Mr. Smith sets himself above the law and rules that give my client the presumption of innocence, and he's here threatening her."

"Sustained," Judge Cassidy says without hesitation.

Mr. Egghead gets visibly irritated and dissatisfied and once again asks Judge Cassidy to speak. He seems to be tired and impatient. "Your Honor, do not believe what this lawyer tells you. At no time did I break the law. I am here to solve the case. My interest is strict in finding out the truth of the events, and of course, if there is a guilty party, this person pays the price for the crimes they committed. If you pay attention, you'll see that her lack of control shows the closer I get to her. It's almost neurotic…"

Mr. Egghead, out of control, points his finger at Ms. O'Brien and continues to say absurd things to her. He starts attacking her in the personal sphere. It's a horror show. He fires several misogynistic attacks, belittles her performance by implying that women don't understand the law, talks about her physical appearance to embarrass her, and uses Ms. O'Brien's recent separation to diminish her—as if women lose their credibility once they no longer have a man by their side. As she coldly listens to Mr. Egghead, she seems to be waiting for him to dig his own grave.

"Mr. Smith," Judge Cassidy interrupts him. "I'm not going to list the amount of nonsense that just came out of your mouth, as I believe you can't process so many character revisions. You shame all of us, people of the law. Do you believe that your role exempts you from responsibilities? Your role is not just to button the handcuffs, convince the jury to put people behind bars, and do it at any cost. You didn't just offend your opponent in this courtroom. You offended all women! I invite you to review all your comments, as they only served to reveal things about yourself and nothing about the case, the accused, or her defense. Well... Let's continue! Ms. O'Brien, would you kindly present your version of events?"

"Yes, Your Honor."

Ms. O'Brien gets up, looks everyone in the eyes, and starts saying, "Ladies and gentlemen, the fact that this girl is sitting here, receiving all these accusations, is already a serious and sad fact to note regarding how our legal system needs a revision. In the wake of an accusation, the justice system is predisposed to believe the accused is innocent until proven guilty. While every case is different, Nora has been subject to heavy accusations, and her right to be presumed innocent until the end of this trial has been revoked. And why do I say this? I say this because everything, absolutely everything, everything depends on justice, depends on the legal order. The impact of an accusation on the life of an innocent person is irreparable. This person may never recover from it, but if that innocent person is a teenage girl, this experience can become a painful and incurable wound of injustice, as she will experience apparent freedom., even if acquitted. My father was killed because he was mistaken for a robber while parking his car to buy bread. Injustice, ladies and gentlemen, is not just about impunity. It also happens when you point the finger or pull the trigger without factual evidence."

A sepulchral silence takes over the courtroom. I look at Judge Cassidy, who seems to approve of Ms. O'Brien's speech. Mr. Egghead has his head down and remains motionless. The attentive audience breathes heavily.

"I call Ruth Guzman, a waitress at Nugfries, to the stand."

Ruth walks in, and I don't quite understand what she's doing there or what she's going to say, but I remember her as the waitress who served us at the cafeteria. I look at Ms. O'Brien, and she holds my hand, asking me to be strong.

Then Ms. O'Brien asks, "Ruth, you waited on the Bailey family on the day of the accident, correct?"

"Yes, I did."

"Could you let us know what you saw?"

"Sure. I was pregnant then, so I frequently went to the cafeteria's bathroom. I found Giovanna crying desperately in the bathroom when the family was there. I went to her and asked if she needed help, but she kept saying that she couldn't take it anymore and that she would put an end to everything. I even asked what happened, but she said many disconnected things. She said she was being harassed and that her husband was in league with "them." I even thought that her husband was doing her some harm. But soon after, she calmed down and said that it was all in her head, that she was without her medications. After that, she returned to her table and looked fine, smiling at her husband, so I thought I didn't have to worry anymore."

"Did you see anything else out of the ordinary that day with the Bailey family?"

Ruth does not hesitate, "I saw Giovanna taking a bottle out of her bag and putting a yellow liquid in her and her husband's soda while their daughter took her milkshake from the counter."

"So you saw Mrs. Bailey pouring some yellow liquid into her and her husband's soda?"

"Yes."

"And can you tell if Mr. Bailey saw his wife pour the yellowish liquid into their drinks?"

"No, he didn't. He was talking on the phone at that moment."

"Did you ever inform anyone, talk to anyone about it?"

"No. As she had talked about not taking medication, I innocently thought it might be it. Only after I saw the case on TV did I begin to suspect something was wrong there."

"Thank you, Ruth. No further questions."

As Ruth returns to her seat, Mr. Smith gets up, goes to Judge Cassidy, and suggests that perhaps the *waitress* has been bribed. Noticing Smith's movement, Ms. O'Brien goes to the judge and asks for the floor once again, "Your Honor, I would like to add that we have given you the footage of the Nugfries Restaurant, in which you can see Mrs. Giovanna Bailey pouring a liquid into her and her husband's glasses."

Ms. O'Brien hands the flash drive with the images to Judge Cassidy.

And then she addresses me, "Nora, I'd like to ask you a few things, all right?"

"Okay."

"Nora, can you recognize the yellowish liquid your mother poured into the glasses?"

"Yes."

"Does it have the characteristics of your parents' poison at home?"

"Yes."

"Did you see your mother pouring the poison into the sodas?"

"No."

When Ms. O'Brien finished the questions, something inside me turned. My eyes remained dry, and I felt like a ruin. I had lost my innocence. It had turned into dust. It was my own mother who did it; that's the verdict. Was she selfish, giving up on life and taking her love with her, leaving me alone? Or am I the problem, the person who couldn't see any suffering or need that wasn't mine? Condemnation is certain! An innocent woman is imprisoned in the truth of events, condemned to know that there is not enough time to pay for liberation and oblivion. What's left for me besides this wound? What's left for me unless the unalterable vacuum that sucks everything into a black hole? I feel angry! I wish she were alive now for me to kill her myself. I wanted at least some justification for the guilt that consumed me.

Judge Cassidy closes the session. Silence fills the courtroom. The jury slowly leaves with their heads down. Ms. O'Brien looks at me and speaks to me cautiously. With tears in their eyes, my uncles Ted and Mark hug me but don't say anything. There is no victory on that day. No joy is possible in the face of tragedy. There's no room for words; there's no peace in me.

As we leave the courtroom, journalists crowd around us and ask countless questions, waiting for some statement after the newest revelations.

"Nora, what do you have to say after finding out that your mother was responsible for your father's death?"

"What do you expect now from the next accusation? Are you confident?"

"What are your next steps regarding the prosecution's accusations?"

I say nothing. I'm not really there, I can't reason, and I feel an incalculable, heavy emptiness flooding everything inside me. And before we could get in the car to head back to the hotel, I noticed Elizabeth and my cousin Eliza approaching us. The policewoman who accompanied us, Mrs. Jones, tries to avoid them getting close, but before we get in the car, Eliza gets rid of obstacles. She gets very close to me and throws rotten eggs at my head. At that moment, a tremendous fury seizes me, and like an animal, I advance on her. Before she can flee, I grab her hair, lay her on the floor, punch her face, and scratch her skin. In a matter of seconds, I make her bleed. It took Mrs. Jones, my uncles Mark and Ted, and even a journalist—who didn't know whether to take photos or help out—to get me off my cousin. Without them, I would have killed Eliza right in front of the cameras, amid journalists and police. They were getting what they wanted from the start, turning me into a monster.

We arrived at the hotel, and after leaving me alone to calm down, Uncle Ted and Uncle Mark approached me to talk. They wanted to know what had happened to me on the farm of Uncle John, my father's brother. That disturbed me so much—they noticed and asked what happened there, with those people, to make me feel completely out of control.

"Do you really want to know? Do you really want to get involved with this?" I ask them both.

Without hesitation, Uncle Ted says, "Nora, you are our daughter now! We need to know what they did to you! And we need to know everything, every detail."

"Are you suspicious of me?" I ask.

They're both embarrassed for a second, but then Uncle Mark takes the lead and says firmly, "No, Nora! We believe in you. But we need answers. We need to know how we can help you."

Chapter Three

Farm - Yellowhammer

When my parents passed away, my paternal family from Alabama was the first to hear the news.

They were waiting for us to arrive at the farm when they heard about a car accident involving a family coming from Florida. It was us. They arrived at the hospital the evening of the same day, but as I was catatonic, the medical staff thought I should rest and see my relatives the next day. This was the day I received the news of my parents' deaths and the beginning of this nightmare.

My father's brother, my uncle John Bailey, and his wife Elizabeth entered the room minutes after Dr. Northon broke the news of my parents' deaths. At that moment, I didn't think twice. My first reaction was to jump out of bed and hug them so tightly that I almost made my Uncle John fall.

I felt like I was in free fall, and hugging them was like finding a safe boat. I held onto the sympathy they offered me. Compassion is easier to find after tragedies, even in those people of dubious character. When they take everything away from you, you accept every little affection others offer you, even if they don't mean it. I couldn't imagine that this decision would lead me to an even worse outcome, with much more suffering and yet another tragedy.

Uncle John and Elizabeth took me "home" to Yellowhammer Farm, where everyone else was waiting for us. My relatives came to me one by one, saying their condolences when I arrived.

"I'm sorry! Welcome."

The last to welcome me was Eliza, my cousin. Before coming to me, she looked at her mother, huffing, and made sure I realized that she was only doing this out of obligation.

Elizabeth, with a forced smile, conducted everyone. They looked like puppets in her hands. I understood she was the boss from day one; she just needed to look at everyone once to get what she wanted. Elizabeth was the law and order of that place, and nothing happened there without her supervision and control.

She was cold, calculating, and cruel. I could feel that my presence irritated her and that the formality of the good reception and the friendliness she insisted on showing would not last long. The help Elizabeth offered me was not real. It was a cheap act for sordid ends; In those lands, I noticed all sorts of strange movements and immediately sensed the danger. Bad people rush to take advantage of you when you are hurt, like vultures. Elizabeth's goal became clear to me as time passed.

My arrival at the Yellowhammer farm somewhat resembled "The Fox and the Lion." The badly hurt fox receives a visit from the Lion, who, claiming to have good intentions, wants to come in to lick the fox's wounds to heal. The very smart and suspicious fox replies that despite believing the lion has virtue, the tongue is close to the teeth. The Fox prefers to bear its pain alone rather than to be devoured by a lion.

Like the fox, I was suspicious of Elizabeth's intentions from day one. I felt she was up to something and that my going there had not been a sign of a good deed and kindness. Elizabeth wanted something—there was already a plan in place, but I didn't know what it was or who else was involved.

I didn't trust anyone—everyone could be my enemy. I felt that they meant me harm. I could feel in the air that something was about to happen and that I was once again alone.

Though a rich man, Uncle John had no voice in the house, and Elizabeth did what she wanted. The orders always came from her, and he always bowed his head. I could feel his unhappiness in his dull, weakened face. I tried to approach him, but Elizabeth made everyone avoid me. Uncle John was forbidden to speak to me, and Elizabeth tried to get his attention whenever he attempted to.

"John, what are you doing there? Come on, come help me!" She said, always finding some excuse.

The same happened with my cousins. They were forbidden to play with me, creating a deep distance between us. Eliza, Asher, and Bob were always together. Eliza was the leader, like her mother. And it didn't take long for them to make fun of me. They threw mud at me, left leaves and tree bark on my bed, ripped my clothes, and nothing happened to them— none of their actions were even reprimanded.

They called me *silly Nora*. They made fun of my way of talking, dressing, and always made me their enemy, even if I didn't do or say anything to them. And despite wanting to strangle them while they slept, I did nothing. I remained firm, without fighting back, without reporting to anyone. I endured it all in silence.

My father's second brother, Uncle Bruce, could do something, but he watched everything and sometimes found it funny. He had always been a quiet man, and we could never know what was going on in his head. But I could tell there was a savagery hidden deep in his eyes. He was a member of Uncle John's family, the brother who never got along with anyone. He was always involved in fights, scandals with ex-girlfriends, and gambling, until Uncle John, who had a lot of possessions, offered him a job at Yellowhammer Farm.

I could tell that Uncle Bruce envied his brother. He looked at John with a dark vibe, like an animal circling its prey, and occasionally when he drank, he blurted out that his brother John was lucky—the only reason he achieved so much.

Uncle Bruce's son, Andrew, had a disability. He couldn't speak very well, his motor functions were visibly impaired, and he had difficulty understanding simple concepts. They all neglected Andrew, and he never received a diagnosis or an answer about how he could be treated. On the contrary, the family always tried to hide him out of shame for his condition.

Uncle Bruce and Andrew lived in a house separated from the farmhouse and seldom attended the parties and get-togethers in the main house. But I couldn't understand that despite Elizabeth's humiliating treatment of Uncle Bruce, he was always chatting with her around Yellowhammer. They had secrets; I could tell by the abrupt way they ended the conversation when anyone approached the two.

Andrew was a lovely child, my only companion. His naivety sometimes revealed something to me about what he heard from Elizabeth and Uncle Bruce.

He said his father had secret business with Miss Elizabeth, but he couldn't tell me. Still, Andrew always hummed the same phrase, "Daddy wants half the orange! Half the orange! Half the orange... But I can't talk, can't talk, can't talk!"

Andrew was the only cousin close to me; all the others were strangers. But we could rarely meet to talk. Elizabeth wouldn't let anyone, even Andrew, get close to me. So Uncle Bruce forbade the boy to speak to me.

And even though I lived in the same house as Andrew and Uncle Bruce, I couldn't talk to them. We had lunch and dinner at different times, and if I moved to sit at the table with them, Uncle Bruce was ready to chase me away. He put me to sleep in the back room, away from all the other rooms in the house. I even used a different bathroom. He and Elizabeth wanted me away from them, away from everyone. They wanted me to stay isolated.

Slowly, Elizabeth started to give me chores. Cook dinner, clean the toilets, feed the chickens. Within thirty days, I was the one that swept the big house, washed everyone's clothes, fed the animals, and cooked the food.

The house was huge, and there was always a massive pile of clothes to wash. The animal food containers weighed a lot, so it was difficult for a single person to do all the chores. But she obliged me, and her children were responsible for patrolling me. They were the ones who dictated the rules; they took advantage of me, and I did everything they were responsible for—schoolwork, repairing personal objects and clothes, and even taking the blame for anything they had done.

But what saddened me the most was not being able to study anymore. Elizabeth forbade me from going to school. According to her, if I continued studying, I couldn't handle my duties at Yellowhammer Farm. So I took advantage of my service to do my cousins' schoolwork, the books they brought from school. That way, I could continue learning on my own. When Elizabeth found out I had access to the books, she forbade me to read. I had to make a deal with my cousins—If they let me read in secret, I could continue doing their schoolwork. Only then was I able to continue my education.

I took the books and homework from Eliza at night and delivered them to her room the next day before dawn.

Of course, it was very difficult after a lot of housework to have the strength to study and do everyone's schoolwork, but I knew that was all I had; knowledge was my only asset, my only weapon.

When my paternal family became responsible for me, my parents' assets were in their possession. My uncle John and Elizabeth, after all, were my legal guardians. So, until I was an adult, I wasn't entitled to anything. And if what little my parents left me was with my uncle John, that meant it was actually with Elizabeth—she owned everything.

On the farm, my work was intense. In addition to taking care of the household chores, doing my cousins' schoolwork, and taking care of the animals, I was also in charge of separating and organizing the toxins to control pests and prevent insects from destroying the peanuts fields. My job was to prepare the toxins for application. Before my arrival, this was one of Elizabeth's children's tasks, the twins Asher and Bob. It was also assigned to me upon my arrival, as were all the other things they didn't like to do.

The twins weren't just alike physically; they were both equally dumb. Although I pitted them, their naivety was an asset to me. They were easily fooled.

I was treated like a slave—I worked for food and a roof over my head, nothing more. I was forbidden to participate in the big house's festivities or go into town to do anything. I was a prisoner. When I needed items for self-care, I had to get them from Eliza.

Eliza was very vain; every weekend, she had to go to the city to take care of her appearance—she had her hair and nails done, and her clothes had to be in perfect condition, completely lined up. She would throw things away or complain if something were even a little off. Ohh, and she complained a lot! Eliza's life was perfect, but she could only see what she didn't have.

For me, what she didn't have, had nothing to do with physical attributes, clothes, or perfect hair, because she had lots of that in abundance. For me, she didn't have the peace of possessing a good heart. Eliza wanted the image of someone good, pure in heart, but she only got the surface. She needed perfection to hide the impurities in her soul that became more cloudy and dark every day. Deep down, I even feel sorry for her; she is just the reflection of her mother, and she had no one to look at. Elizabeth was Eliza's role model, and she wouldn't know how to be different from that.

The Yellowhammer farm was partly a peanut plantation and the other part a forest reservation. The reserve was my refuge. I don't know if I inherited this characteristic from my parents, but I felt very well when surrounded by trees, plants, and animals. When I had some time, I would always go into the woods and stay there for hours. I felt more protected there than with people, even my relatives—especially my relatives, who I considered enemies more than family.

I kept thinking that if a hurricane came and I could save someone, I would only save my cousin Andrew. He was as much a victim as I was. All the others, I would love to see them blown away by the wind, especially Elizabeth and Eliza—who was a true copy of her mother.

One day at the big house, they made several large chocolate cakes to welcome Uncle John and Elizabeth's friends over the weekend. I could smell the cake several meters away from the house, and I, who hadn't eaten any sweets for a long time, had the bright idea to steal a piece of the cake for myself once the guests left. I didn't ask for it because I was sure Elizabeth would forbid me to eat. Well, I did all my work. I tidied up the house for the arrival of the visitors, took care of the animals, locked up the dogs, and when I finished everything, I stayed hidden, watching everyone under a tree near the big house, where they wouldn't notice me.

The night seemed endless. It felt as if the visitors would never leave. My belly wouldn't stop growling, and I couldn't stop imagining that soft chocolate cake in my mouth, with the chocolate syrup running on my lips. The wait was so long that I sat at the foot of the tree to wait and fell asleep. When I woke up, it was late at night, and the moon and stars were already lighting up the sky. But when I looked at the big house again, I saw that the visitors' cars were still there, which meant, to my dismay, that the visitors hadn't left yet and that they might take a long time.

I stayed there under that starry sky with a full moon illuminating me, waiting anxiously for a piece of cake. That made me understand a lot about how small things can have the power to make someone happy. In my case, it was just a piece of cake; that was the only thing I wanted. But I feared that the visitors would sleep in, and I wouldn't be able to carry out my plan.

So I started to pray to God that they would go away that night. While I asked the lord to take them away, they were still there, eating, drinking, talking, laughing out loud... And, of course, they would still be there for a long time.

But I had faith on my side, so I asked, "I'm going to go to Uncle Bruce's house to get a cloth to wrap the cake, and when I get back, they'll be gone."

When I arrived at Uncle Bruce's house, I found my cousin Andrew on the porch waiting for me, "Where were you, Nora-Nora?"

"I went to the big house," I answered.

"Were you at the party? Drew wanted to go to the party with you! Why didn't you take Drew along?"

"No! I was not, Drew. I just went to see if I could... Never mind!"

I stop, dismayed at what I had just done for a piece of cake. It was such a small thing for them and a big one for me... That injustice was starting to eat me inside out.

"Nora-Nora, are you mad at Drew?"

"No, Drew! I'm just tired," I answered.

"Drew is tired, too."

We stood there for a few minutes in silence, and before I gave up on returning to the big house to get a piece of the cake, I obstinately lifted my head and asked Andrew, "Would you like a piece of chocolate cake?"

"Drew doesn't have money to buy a cake! But I would like to have one," He said, licking his lips.

"You don't need money, Drew! But you'll have to help me get it, will you?"

"Okay!" Andrew said with excitement.

The motivation to get the chocolate cake from the big house became even stronger, more than a challenge—getting the cake was now a mission. Andrew would have fun with me that night.

"Go to the kitchen and get a big white cloth from the third drawer of the red cabinet and bring it to me, Drew."

Andrew went into the kitchen and brought two pieces of cloth.

"I don't need two, one was more than enough, Drew."

"One is for your cake, and the other is for mine! We are two people."

I looked at him fondly and nodded in agreement. Andrew, despite his condition, is much smarter than the idiot twins and the obtuse princess. I look at him and agree with our plan.

"Drew, I'll go there, and you wait for me here, in your room, so your father won't suspect anything, okay?"

"Drew can't tell him?"

"No, you can't! This is our secret,"

"Okay, Drew won't tell anyone. But what about cousins Bob and Asher?" He asks.

"No one, Andrew!" I answered.

"Not Aunt Elizabeth, Uncle John, and Cousin Eliza?" He insists.

"Especially to them, you shouldn't tell anyone! Only you and I will know! Okay?"

"Yeah! Drew knows how to keep secrets."

"Then go to your room, and if all goes well, I'll meet you there in a little while with our cakes."

Andrew nodded confidently and ran off to his room. With the white pieces of cloth in my hands, I went on my mission, hoping that the visitors were gone and that there was plenty of cake left.

Arriving there, I saw that the visitors' cars were gone and that it was time to act. And in a mix of sensations, I approached the kitchen surreptitiously. I felt euphoric and anxious at the same time; after all, I was afraid of being caught. My sense of guilt also took hold of me, and for a moment, I stopped. But I didn't give up and continued, even though my hands were sweating. I climbed the stairs at the back of the house and entered, making my way to the kitchen without making a sound. I heard Elizabeth and Uncle John talking in the living room. The wooden floor started to creak as I walked on tiptoe, so I tried to be more careful and distribute my weight on the floor. I heard the twins fighting in the hallway by the kitchen door, disputing which of the two would kiss a high school girl named Sophia. Finally, I opened the kitchen door very carefully not to make any noise as I went inside.

The kitchen's lights were off, but I could see well because of the moonlight coming through the window. There were two glass plates with cake on the table. I went to them with extraordinary joy—I couldn't resist; I dipped my finger in the chocolate syrup desperately, as if it were my first meal after days of deprivation. As I wrapped the pieces of cake in my cloth, I could already picture Andrew's joy when he saw our cakes and how happy that night would be for us. *A happy night at last, amid so much suffering,* I thought to myself. I was almost crying; I was so pleased with those pieces of cake and the fact that I could carry out that mission. That little treat made me feel good...

When I finished wrapping the pieces of cake, I thought, "How about a soda? Soda wouldn't be a bad idea." So I went to the fridge and grabbed a soda to take with me as well.

But when I closed the fridge door while still holding the wrapped pieces of cake in one hand and the two-liter soda bottle in my left hand… Eliza opened the kitchen door, turned on the light, got scared, and after understanding what I was doing there, she decided to report me and screamed, calling her mother, "Mother! Mother! Mother! Mother!"

I ran towards her to escape through the door, but she grabbed me by the arms and continued to make a fuss calling for Elizabeth, who arrived terrified in the kitchen, followed by Uncle John and then the twins. Elizabeth walked over to me and took the cake and the soda bottle out of my hands.

"What is it? Is that the manners we're teaching you, Nora? This is what barbaric people do. I'm not raising you for you to turn against us. You're a thief."

"She even tried to run away, mom! If it weren't for me holding her here, she'd be gone by now," Eliza said.

Elizabeth thanked her daughter and continued to scold me, "Stealing food, Nora! What an ugly thing to do! You're getting worse every day, without any manners, so you must stay away from here, living with the others. Why didn't you ask me if you wanted a piece of cake?"

"You wouldn't give it to me!" I answered.

"Of course I would," she said.

"Then let me go with these pieces of cake. I don't need the soda," I begged.

Elizabeth walked around me, circling me, until she stood behind me and put her hands on my shoulders, speaking in my ear, "My child, you can't do this anymore. This isn't good behavior! So you'll have to learn the hard way. You won't take anything from here."

At that moment, Eliza laughed with satisfaction while I cried copiously. While I was crying, Elizabeth went on, trying to justify the unjustifiable, speaking to the winds, "And besides, cake is not healthy! Eliza even ate a tiny slice herself because of her diet. You should follow her example, Nora. Start taking care of yourself more, have some vanity. All that cake, plus soda, is a bomb for your body. One day you will thank me!"

As Elizabeth spoke, I ran out of there sobbing with tears. I couldn't understand how anyone could be as mean as she was. I just wanted a piece of cake! A piece of cake and maybe a soda, that wasn't much. To her, it was nothing.

On the way back to Uncle Bruce's house, running around bewildered by what had just happened, I tripped over a rock and got covered in mud—as if I hadn't suffered enough humiliation. When I entered my room, I lay down, smeared with mud, and curled up in a fetal position. I cried painfully. I felt every part of my body ache, every memory of that night— the wait in the tree, the prayer, the hope I gave Andrew... The joy of having the cake in my hands, the hostile attitude of Eliza and Elizabeth. I was deeply saddened.

Hearing me cry, Andrew went to my room. He stood by my door for a few seconds, then walked over to me and asked, "You didn't get the cake, Nora-Nora?"

"No!" I answered, still crying.

"Don't be like that! Drew doesn't want to see Nora-Nora crying!"

"It's okay, Drew! Just leave me alone for a bit," I answered

"Drew will do that. Drew will do it…"

Andrew left the room, and I stayed there crying for hours, curled up, feeling a lot of pain all over my body, but mainly in my chest. This pain continued until tiredness started to get me down, and I fell asleep.

Early the next day, I was awakened by heavy, clumsy footsteps beside my bed. When I opened my eyes and looked at my feet, I saw two boots completely covered in mud. I soon realized it was Andrew. He had both hands holding our pieces of cloth with the slices of cake inside. I looked at his face, and he was grinning from ear to ear.

"Andrew! What is that?" I asked.

"The chocolate cakes!" He answered.

"I know, but who gave it to you?"

"Nobody gave it to me, I got it for us. Drew wants to see Nora-Nora happy! Are you happy?" He asked.

Andrew made a genuine gesture. Sometimes the goodness of some gives us strength to resist the evil of others. "Yes, I'm happy! You made me very happy, Andrew!"

"Only our secret is no longer a secret. Uncle John saw me take it! I told him I needed to get the cloth back because we would need them. You're not mad at me, are you?"

"Of course not! You are very smart, Andrew! Thank you very much!"

And so after a turbulent night, in the first rays of sun in the morning, Andrew and I had our fill of the chocolate cake that was really, really delicious.

But the sweetness of the cake did not fix the bitterness in my mouth, the harshness of indifference, disgust, and unmeasured cruelty, which that family practiced against me every day. Elizabeth's cynicism, Eliza's sarcasm, Uncle John's insensitivity, the twins' disinterest, and their lack of empathy prevailed. All those ungrateful and sterile faces of love, virtue, and compassion mingled and hovered in my head throughout the next few days.

I became more and more miserable as the days passed. There was a sense of ruin and dust within me, indicating that I was someone who had been at war. Little by little, they killed everything good in me, my naivety, my hope, and my dreams. Before them, I thought that the worst that could happen to me was to lose the most important people in my life, but that wasn't enough for them; they wanted to see me broken. I was their target, someone that channeled all their hatred, all their damnation. I had no one for me but myself.

A few months later, when I thought they couldn't take anything else away from me, they proved they could be even worse.

Halloween was just around the corner, and Yellowhammer Farm was responsible for providing the pumpkins for parties across town. It was a period of hard work on the farm. There was the harvesting of the pumpkins, then the cleaning process, sorting them into different sizes, and organizing the pumpkins by categories before they were taken to the city.

Elizabeth and Uncle John were people of respect. Everyone knew them. Elizabeth had plans to enter politics, and she forced Uncle John to participate in various charity events so the local people could always see the family name favorably. Halloween was when they received more prestige because of the pumpkin donations and the charity events they supported throughout the city. But only I knew that underneath all that apparent goodness, they were putrid people with corroded souls who only helped others out of self-interest.

Halloween had always been special to me. It wasn't just an excuse to wear monster costumes and go out trick or treating. Of course, I loved that part too, but Halloween, for me, meant much more. It represented the union between my parents and me. We'd never spent any Halloween apart, my parents met at a Halloween party, and I was born on the thirty-first of October. So it was always a date of celebration, love, and happiness for us—a date we celebrated our family.

So even as I tried to internally deny any involvement with the date while I was living on the Yellowhammer farm, my heart clamored to participate in the smallest details of the party preparations. A heart that wants to bloom isn't hindered by the reasons it cannot do so.

I actively participated in all the work on the farm for the Halloween party, which was also my birthday. I was very involved, and it all started to have a greater meaning. It was as if I was doing it for my parents as they watched. And then my badass pose, my frown, it was suddenly gone. That was when Eliza and the twins approached me with a niceness I'd never seen before. Of course I was suspicious, but I was so emotionally available that I just didn't care what my sense of danger told me. I simply allowed myself to be vulnerable and told them my birthday would be on Halloween. And then Eliza, after ordering me to sew her and the twins' costumes, invited me to go to a party with them.

"Me, go to the party with you?"

"Yes, it's your birthday, isn't it?" Eliza said.

My heart filled with joy, and I got excited about the idea, despite having my danger sensor going off in my head. I couldn't stop imagining what it would be like and how happy a party would make me.

"But Eliza, your mother wouldn't let me go with you!" I said in a sad tone.

Eliza looked at the twins before saying confidently, "We'll convince her, won't we, boys?"

"Yeah! Yeah!" The twins responded together.

"Would you do this for me, Eliza?" I asked with complicity.

"Of course, we are cousins, Nora! Why shouldn't I do my cousin a kindness? I'm a good person!"

"I would be very happy if you could convince your mother to let me go with you to the Halloween party, Eliza."

"All right, all right! Now finish our costumes because if we don't have costumes by the thirty-first, neither you nor we will be able to join the party," Eliza said hastily and pragmatically.

So I rushed to produce our costumes. Eliza was going to be a corpse bride, the twins would be vampires, and I wanted to go in the traditional witch costume with a hat, broom, and wand. I spent the whole week working on preparations during the day and the outfits at night. It was a very tiring week, but I always thought I would be rewarded for my hard work. I would leave the farm for the first time and go to the city with them.

The first costume I started to make was that of Eliza, which took the most work due to the wealth of details that she insisted on demanding. Then I made the costumes for the Twins who wanted to be identical because they wanted to trick people by impersonating each other. And finally, at the dawn of the thirtieth day, when all the costumes were ready except mine, I started to dedicate myself to producing what I would wear for Halloween. I wouldn't be able to make the clothes I wanted in the short time I had left, but I was still so excited that I was going to a party on my birthday. Despite the lack of time, my witch costume was beautiful. The hat was purple, and the black dress had a button-up neck. The wand was a stick I found on the farm, and I would make it even better with charcoal makeup. I had limited resources, but I made it work.

At the end of the day, after I'd given them the costumes and finished my chores, I started dressing up for the Halloween party in town. While I was getting ready, Andrew knocked on my bedroom door, "Hi, Nora-Nora!"

"Hi, Drew. I'm in a bit of a hurry, okay? So if you need anything, just let me know, and I'll do it for you later."

"No, I don't need anything! Drew heard that Nora-Nora was having a birthday, so he came to bring these flowers he picked up in our garden."

"Oh! You didn't have to, Drew. Thank you very much! Would you put the flowers on the bed!"

Andrew put the flowers on the bed and watched me pass the charcoal around my eyes.

"What is Nora-Nora doing? She's getting scary!"

"That's the intention, Drew. It's Halloween!"

Andrew looked suspiciously at me.

"Do you know what Halloween is, Drew?" I asked.

"Drew is afraid of Halloween."

"You don't have to be afraid. It's just a date to play at being different."

Andrew sat on the bed with the flowers beside him and looked thoughtful.

"What happened, Drew?" I asked.

"Drew feels like every day is Halloween."

"How come?"

"Drew is different from everyone else every day."

I felt a little disconcerted by Andrew's reasoning and sat next to him. I wanted him to see how special his being different made him.

"Drew, being different does not make you worse than anyone! You are precious to me, smarter, and purer in your heart and soul than all of us put together. So you're not different because you're bad. You're different, and you're the best of us all!"

"Is Drew the best?"

"Yes, the best!"

"Better than cousin Asher and cousin Bob?"

"Much better than cousin Asher and cousin Bob."

"Better than Nora-Nora?"

"Yes, much better than me! Now let me finish getting ready because soon-soon I have to leave!"

I got up, went to the mirror, and continued to get ready. Andrew followed me.

"Where are you going, Nora-Nora?"

"I'm going to the Halloween party downtown." I could see that Andrew was still confused. "What is it, Drew?"

"Who's Nora-Nora going with?" He asked me.

"With Aunt Elizabeth, Uncle John, and cousins Eliza, Asher, and Bob," I answered him, noticing he still had a confused look. "Something wrong, Drew?"

"They're gone already!"

"What?" I asked.

"Before Drew came to bring Nora-Nora the flowers, he was loading the boxes into Aunt Elizabeth's car."

"Boxes, which boxes?" I asked

"Aunt Elizabeth's boxes."

When I came to my senses, I ran out onto the porch, and from there, I saw that their car was no longer there. They had left me behind.

Andrew came to me, "See? They're gone."

I suddenly turned around and answered Andrew stupidly, almost yelling at him, "I see that, Andrew! I'm not blind, okay? I can see!"

My heart was racing, my face was red as a tomato, the vein in my forehead was bulging, and I started to writhe in rage and scream. I took off my shoes, threw them away, ripped the hat with my nails—the hat I had spent all night making—and left it on the driveway. I ran towards the fields, and Andrew tried to stop me by running after me.

"Nora-Nora! Where are you going?"

"Leave me alone, Andrew! I need to be alone!"

"But Nora-Nora, it is getting dark! It's dangerous."

"Leave me, Andrew!"

Andrew got behind little by little while I went deeper into the fields. I was crying out of rage, and I felt my skin curl. I got the wooden wand I had made and started to hurt my arms, legs, and nails, and before I knew it, I was completely immersed in the middle of the trees. I found a rock to sit on and stayed there feeling like the saddest, loneliest person in the world. I imagined Eliza having fun on Halloween in the beautiful costume I made, with Elizabeth at her side. I imagined the twins stuffing themselves with candy and thinking they were the bigwigs in the vampire capes I'd cut out and sewn. I pictured Uncle John with his dull face, following Elizabeth's orders blindly.

It was my birthday, and there I was, in that swamp, hoping that some monstrous creature would appear to put an end to my misery. I trully wished something bad would happen to me.

My inner voice gave way to the terrifying sounds of the fields at night. Sounds of owls, crickets, birds, crawling animals, and the winds shook the branches of the trees. Everything was happening around me, and I felt smaller, vulnerable, and unimportant to the world.

At that moment, a light the size of a grain of rice appeared in the middle of the trunk of a leafy tree. This light was flashing and mesmerizing; it came and went as if testing my courage.

Despite my fear, I stood there, staring at the tree trunk. And then, that little bright blue-tinted light began to wander around me, and I couldn't take my eyes off it. It seemed harmless to me and even had a playful vibe, which distracted me from everything else and made me forget the sadness that had made a home inside me.

The tiny light started to wander through the fields, and I followed it. It was dancing amusingly. It twirled and created shapes of flowers, animals, and insects in the air. It fell to the ground, dripped along the path, then took off again, dancing in the air. I kept following it. Soon, it felt like we had created a universe of our own. I followed the light everywhere with euphoria, as if under a spell. I was no longer alone or afraid.

At one point, the tiny light bumped into a flower. It withered under the light's touch, making me stop suspiciously. The small light, realizing what it had just done to the flower, looked back at me suspiciously and then began to withdraw. The light became thinner, and it seemed like it knew it was losing its charm. It approached me, now not as bright, and said goodbye in a shy, embarrassed way.

The light went away, and I thought it would disappear completely. But when it was almost vanishing, it decided to increase in size and reveal its true form. The light illuminated the fields, and before my eyes, that tiny light turned into a huge moose. The same moose I saw at the hospital, and maybe the same one that appeared to my mother in the accident.

A bright blue light surrounded its entire body, which seemed to be made of crystals, like its paws and eyes. Despite all the astonishment that that creature's appearance had already caused me, seeing its transformation before my eyes made me understand that I was not at risk.

Realizing that I hadn't run away after seeing it in its true form, the moose glared at me and shook its antlers as a sign of intimacy and bonding. Like me, that creature only possessed itself and had only solitude for company.

The creature was doing its job without realizing that I was still following it. The moose stopped to touch a bird, which upon being touched, laid down and closed its eyes as if sleeping until the air disappeared out of its body.

Then, with its body shrunken, the creature almost accidentally approached a rabbit that, enchanted by the shapes and colors of the moose, remained motionless there to receive the mortal touch of one of its paws.

As I followed, the dazzling animal continued to walk, and before it took the life of a frog on the bank of a stream, it became aware of my presence. Embarrassed, the Moose lowered its head, sat up, and let the frog take its course.

Intrigued by the radiant magic of the animal and interested in extinguishing my pain, I approach the creature for a mortal embrace to meet my parents. But sensing my intentions, the moose immediately recoiled back, falling into the stream. When I realized I had caused the animal's fall, I went after it and tried to help it. Yet, the moose soon recovered, pulling his paws and telling me *no* with its eyes. It shook its antlers negatively and splashed water on me so I wouldn't get any closer.

Giving up the lunges toward death, I left the stream, sat on its bank, and started to cry. The Moose, noticing my sadness, came towards me and started making funny movements to make me feel good again. It soon realized it couldn't change my mood, so it lay down beside me, keeping me company. After a while, I decided to get up and go back home, but as I had walked a lot through the fields and high trees, I couldn't find my way back.

I decided to spend the night under a pine tree with the creature by my side. I fell asleep thinking that all I had just seen was a delirium of mine, pure imagination. But as soon as I woke up with the first rays of sunlight in the morning, I looked at my side, and the creature was still there, looking at me, and I knew it had not left me alone through the night.

The strange thing is that I felt that it had always been present in my life. But it was only from that moment on that I could see and feel its presence intimately. I continued with all my problems, living that difficult life, but I felt energized and no longer afraid of the future.

Before the moose showed me the way back home, it took me to an apple tree, so I could get something to eat. There we gorged ourselves on the fruit. And with a full belly, I said goodbye to the creature and made my way back home.

Arriving at Uncle Bruce's house, I didn't find anyone there. Andrew, who is always up first thing in the morning, wasn't there. Uncle Bruce, who always asked me to fix him something to eat, was also gone. After the night I had, those absences in the morning meant something bad had happened, and I should be careful because anything and everything that went slightly beyond the "normal" always ended up being my fault.

I decided to see what was happening at the Yellowhammer farm's big house. I took off the filthy costume, took a shower, and changed to get minimally presentable there and not be scolded by Elizabeth. Yet, as I got closer to the house, I could already see several police cars and an ambulance in front of the house. A yellow ribbon encircled the entire place with a *do not trespass* sign.

I saw Elizabeth in tears by the front door, hugging her children. Andrew was sitting with his head down on the stairs. I sneaked up to Andrew and asked him what had happened.

He responded with his eyes on the floor, traumatized, "Killed, killed."

"Who was killed, Andrew?"

"Uncle John! He's inside with the cops around him. We cannot enter, Nora-Nora. There's a lot of blood!"

"Where is your father, Andrew?"

"He went... I don't know where he went!"

At that moment, Elizabeth noticed my presence, and from between the twins' arms, she gave me an evil look. She whispered something I couldn't hear, then smiled at the corner of her mouth just for me to see it. Everyone else can only know the desperation she continued to pretend afterward.

That nasty smile and that look would never fade away from my memory. Elizabeth planned everything perfectly. The plan to kill her husband, my uncle John, began when I stepped foot on the farm. The secret conversations between her and Uncle Bruce, everything, absolutely everything, was meticulously planned. She just needed to convince everyone that it was me who had killed her husband.

First, she started to cast suspicion on me, saying that I was the only one who could have a disagreement with my uncle John because of my working conditions and not adapting to life on the farm. Since I was absent when the whole thing happened, I wasn't there when Uncle John was found. Elizabeth had stayed in town with her kids, claiming she would sort out Yellowhammer's bureaucratic things in the morning. The only one to return to Yellowhammer that night was Uncle John. She had the perfect alibi.

However, her accomplice was my uncle Bruce, who was seen as a very quiet and focused man, but who felt uncontrollable envy toward his brother. He was at the farm when it all happened.

To me, he was the killer who murdered Uncle John in cold blood. He was the only one who couldn't look me in the eye and accuse me of the crime. The man who, after killing his own brother, still moved into his house and lay in his bed.

Elizabeth invited him to go there, claiming she felt unprotected after the attempt on her husband. To this day, she does not reveal that she has an affair with Uncle Bruce, but who knows how long Elizabeth and Uncle Bruce have been together?

It's not difficult to link one thing to the other. Uncle John had possessions, and it would all pass onto her, Elizabeth. So Bruce, who has always envied Uncle John, agrees to the perfidious plan and ends his own brother's life, afterward keeping his wife, money, and possessions.

I didn't know how to prove it at the trial, but I hoped Ms. O'Brien had a plan.

After Uncle Bruce went to live in the big house with Elizabeth, and the investigations started to go forward, Elizabeth needed to point the finger more emphatically at me because if they found out it was Bruce, they would get to her as the mastermind of the crime, it was a matter of time. So she kicked me out of the Yellowhammer farm, and I went to live with my maternal grandparents, Tony and Maria Bell, in Texas, already under threats of being formally charged and arrested for the death of Uncle John.

For my accusation to be credible, Elizabeth had to find someone with similar interests as she did. And there was no one better than the well-known Mr. Egghead. Then the whole legal process began, so my uncertainties about having a normal life. Elizabeth had always been a very influential woman, so she started to involve all the media in the story, inventing a narrative that would stick against me.

I became a mere pawn in their hands, and my chances began to get smaller and smaller. The first news I remember watching was Elizabeth saying that she had filed the accusation against me. She made a scene and cried along with her children and Uncle Bruce. He kept his head down as if he wanted to avoid the cameras.

Numerous investigations were carried out at the Yellowhammer farm to identify the possible person responsible for that heinous crime. But the police accountable for investigating the case were constantly favoring Elizabeth. So it would be very difficult for me to have a fair investigation. It would be difficult to obtain proof of my innocence when the police could be responsible for planting evidence to incriminate me.

They even investigated the bruises on my arms, trying to find my uncle John's DNA there, but nothing was found as I had nothing to do with what had happened to him. Luckily, the laboratory that carried out the exam did not attempt to plant the evidence, and I could wait for the process in freedom.

Others were not so ethical, and police found my fingerprints at the crime scene, my shoes near the house, and my costume hat at the crime scene. But as they didn't find the weapon, the process was in progress, and they waited for more concrete data to put me in jail for good. To me, jail would be just a location; the media already condemned me.

These procedures were all very time-consuming, a lot of false evidence appeared, and many things that had nothing to do with the case started to make a difference in how the media portrayed me. One of these things was my parents' deaths from poisoning. They linked one thing to the other, and on the news, in the newsstands, there was no talk of anything else.

The adjectives on the cover of the magazines were the most alarmist, "The Evil Daughter," "The Killer Girl," "Florida Cancer," "The Alabama Terror," "The Devil's Daughter," and "Evil Comes to Texas." When my grandparents opened their doors for me, they opened the doors to a hurricane that would shake their peaceful lives and leave everything out of place. Wherever I went at that moment in my life, I would take with me my story, my marks, and the overwhelming weight of the lies they told about me. This weight flooded every path I took, and no one in my life could get away with how they made me monstrous.

Chapter Four

Here Now

In Marshall, Texas, I wasn't welcomed with open arms.

My grandmother Maria and my grandfather, Tony Bell, valued anonymity, but that just ended with my arrival. My stay there didn't last long, just three months. But it was enough for a lot of bad things to happen.

My grandfather, Tony, was an ex-combatant in the Vietnam War in 1972, a very rigid man with many war wounds—alcoholism was one of them. My grandfather was an aggressive man, hunted by ghosts from the past, and that was worse when he drank. He was always babbling some nonsense thing, putting on his uniform every Sunday to sit at the breakfast table, assembling and disassembling his gun.

My grandmother was subjected to the excesses of a disturbed man. She was not free to choose anything for the house, much less for herself. In the many times my grandfather Tony beat me, just as he beat Uncle Ted, before sending him away, my grandmother Maria could do nothing but watch and suffer with me. Any attempt at defense would result in an even greater misfortune. My grandmother was a hostage who lived with her executioner for many years. She always had to put up with his temper alone; she smothered her pain at having her son thrown out of the house by his own father, and she had to accept it like that. It was either that or watching my grandfather kill my uncle, as he had sworn he would.

When a man is like that, and there are easy powerless targets around him, he will definitely shoot. That is what happened. My grandfather believed what the media was saying about me, and it didn't take long until I went from an innocent teenager to a guilty woman in his head. And when he was upset, the only thing I could do was lock myself in my room and wait for him to get tired or fall asleep. He would beat me for any reason—being early, being late, leaving the light on, leaving the light up, if the food was too hot and if it was too cold.

Everything, absolutely everything, was an excuse for him to give me a taste of his cruelty.

Many things happened to me in Marshall, Texas, that I would like to forget, but I returned to school there. First, it was very difficult to find a school that would accept me since, with the repercussions of the case gaining national notoriety, no one would like to receive a "criminal" of my stature in their school.

My grandmother was about to give up when I asked her to let me speak to the headmaster of the last possible school in the area so that he would let me continue my education. His name was Mr. Collins, and he was the headmaster at Texas College High School.

"We have no vacancies!" He said as we arrived. "The rooms are packed! We can't take anyone else!"

But he didn't expect me to be so relentless. I managed to get him to listen to my story. First, he heard all the reasons why I should be accepted—My grades in Florida, my commitment to school, and my interest in getting a degree. When I realized nothing I said had any effect, I appealed to frankness and spoke about the accusations.

"Mr. Collins, I know you don't want to accept me here because you think I'm guilty of those crimes. But the truth is, I have nothing to do with all of that. I was deprived of education for almost a year. That family kept me their prisoner, forced me to work for them, and now they are accusing me of that crime. I'm just asking you for a chance, a month. A month for you to get to know me and decide for yourself if I can continue or not."

My eyes were dull with tears, my voice was choked, and I made him believe that I wouldn't leave until I managed to get back to school. And even though he got annoyed, thinking about the various problems the school would attract with my presence, Mr. Collins agreed.

"One month! Just a month, girl. And know that you will have to leave if things get worse."

That sounded like music to my ears. I left the meeting ecstatic; I thought, "*My life is finally getting back on track. This opportunity to go back to school is just the beginning. I will be able to have friends, and I will work. I will have a profession. I will be useful to the world. My life will gain meaning.*"

But my excitement was short-lived. The media attacks worsened, and my living situation became even more unbearable. My grandfather started beating me to get me to confess that I was to blame for the death of his daughter, my mother.

He became obsessed with it, and I was subjected to interrogations every day, as soon as I returned from school. When he was drunk, I was even tortured—so that he would get to the "truth" of what had actually happened.

Going to school became challenging. I tried to hide the bruises on my body, but no makeup was good enough to hide the ones on my face. With the bruises on my face taking days to heal and fade away, my grandfather forbade me from going to school. The constant absences and pressure from the media made Mr. Collins expel me.

Forty-five days, that's how long my student dream lasted. And once again, I was a prisoner in my own life. Once again, I was adrift, at the mercy of a lunatic.

When the torture session started, my grandmother would lock herself in the bathroom. She always saw me come out of the garage bruised and with such a hurt look; she understood perfectly well how much that violence was tearing me up inside. My grandmother Maria believed in me and my innocence, but she was afraid to report my grandfather because he was always threatening her. Living with him was living with the gun to our heads twenty-four hours a day. And this was no mere metaphor. He was always armed.

With my processes going on, everything was even more delicate. Contrary to what I expected, my presence in Marshall, Texas, only brought more suffering to my grandmother and me. And things would only get worse before they got better.

At the beginning of the third month of living with my grandparents in Texas, my grandfather started to lock me up in the house's garage. He used shackles to bind my feet and subjected me to a starvation regimen that he said was meant to make me confess all my crimes. This happened at least three times a week, and he would pray to God, asking for forgiveness before and after his torture sessions. I didn't believe he felt any guilt. Those deeds could only come from a truly sick man.

I tried to run away three times. All of these attempts caused me to have even worse consequences during his torture sessions. I was on the verge of confessing that I killed my mother and my uncle to get him to stop. I even wrote several notes asking for help, threw them through the house's windows, and put them in the garbage bag, but none of my efforts had any effect. In the end, my grandmother was quite weakened. She couldn't bear to see what was happening to me. She had a mental breakdown and didn't respond to almost anything; she stopped interacting with everyone and spent her days locked in her room, waiting for death to come.

My grandfather got sick in the middle of the third month I was living with them. He had a lung disease that worsened. From that day on, I was no longer beaten. I became responsible for cooking for everyone. But even when my grandfather was weak, he always monitored me. He always kept his gun with him in case I tried to take advantage of his state and escape.

Those were dark days.

I don't know if it was my luck—or my grandfather's bad luck—when it was near the last day of the third month that I was there, I dreamed that my friend, the moose, with his huge antlers, was breaking down the front door of the house to save me. And the next day, a gas leak in the shower in their bedroom suite caused him and my grandmother to asphyxiate in their sleep. As I was locked in the garage, I only realized that something had happened when it was time for my grandfather to release me so I could cook, and he still hadn't shown up yet.

So I started screaming, first calling him, and then, understanding that he would not come to me, I started screaming for help. It took a few hours before someone passing on the street could hear me and call for help.

The craziest thing about it is that Elizabeth used my grandarents' deaths as a sinister plot to incriminate me even further. She said I had planned everything from start to finish, including the accidental death of my grandparents, to make everyone feel sorry for me.

I would have to be an evil genius, or a psychopath, as Elizabeth is, to come up with something so diabolical. And I'm far from it. I'm just a girl who yearns like no one else for a normal, simple life with no fuss or spotlight.

It is difficult for me not to yearn for revenge. It's easy to enumerate all the legitimate reasons I could have killed my grandfather and uncle. But I didn't do it. I wasn't responsible for their deaths.

I'm not a saint or someone who offers the other cheek. I'm not that. I am someone whose reality and the rawness of things do not respect pre-established rules.

Some things are so bitter they cannot be explained. Some things turn into a stain on the fabric of our souls, an incurable stain that escapes our eyes. Perhaps this story is my redemption, long-awaited freedom, and way toward a fresh start.

Chapter Five

Day 4 - Judgment

At the courthouse door, there is a thirsty huddle of journalists talking about nothing other than Eliza's beating.

The consequences of my impulsive attitude begin to emerge. Everyone now sees my aggressiveness. It is the trigger that the media needed to justify all their false allegations against me. Now everyone can see the "monster" that I am. And although I enjoyed doing what I did, I understand the saying "evil for evil" can't solve the pain I feel. My attitude only fueled the fire with gasoline, and the only one getting burnt was me.

My Uncle Ted and Mark talk to Ms. O'Brien in court as I watch everyone. We all await the arrival of Judge Cassidy. Mr. Egghead is concentrated at his desk, reviewing the prosecution's files and occasionally scratching his shiny bald head.

"Stand up, everyone," says the Judge, and we obey. "Today, we will continue with Nora Bailey's trial. We're going to deal with the charge of the murder of John Bailey, who was killed in the early hours of the first of November of the year before last, fourteen months ago. I request the indictment's formulation so we can proceed with this trial. Mr. Smith, please take it from here."

Mr. Egghead, with short steps like a penguin, takes the center of the court and speaks to the audience, "Ladies and Gentlemen, we have gathered here again today for the clarification of yet another sordid crime committed by this girl who goes by the name of Nora Bailey. My name is Kurt Smith, and in addition to being an assistant attorney for the state of Alabama and representing the people in this courtroom, I am here for John Bailey, an honorable, hardworking family man whose life was taken by a heartless monster. Believe it or not, ladies and gentlemen, it wasn't enough for Nora to coldly kill her uncle while he slept. The other day, leaving this courtroom, Nora cowardly attacked John's daughter, her cousin, Eliza Bailey. Fortunately, Miss Eliza is doing well and will have no permanent after-effect. But such an act cannot go unpunished and will be added to this case by attributing responsibility for such violence to Nora. Ladies and gentlemen, Nora delivered fifteen blows to her cousin's face in front of this courtroom, and it took the strength of three men to remove her from the victim. That shows us the range of her hatred for this family that welcomed her and did her good when she needed it the most."

Ms. O'Brien listens to everything, taking notes, while Mr. Egghead looks at me vicariously.

"And if there was any doubt that Nora was strong enough to crack a man's skull with a baseball bat, that doubt has already been clarified. Someone with the strength to fight three men is strong enough to do this."

At that moment, Mr. Egghead starts showing the images of my Uncle John's body at the crime scene to everyone in the courtroom. These images shock us all; we can see blood in every direction in the room, and his face is completely disfigured.

To the content of the images Mr. Egghead exhibits in the courtroom, some people turn their heads, others lower their heads, and others, unable to bear it, leave the room.

"As you can see, only an animal would be capable of something like this. Only someone very far removed from God would be able to commit such barbarism."

Pointing to the numbered circles in the photographs of the bloodstains in the room, Mr. Egghead continues, "Look right here, at circle number one, and then at circles two, three, and four. The splash of blood projected on the wall follows a defined course and shows us that the accused delivered the first blow here. The victim dragged himself here and, finally, lifeless, ended up here, where we can see this larger pool of blood. This entire blood path, Your Honor, was calculated by experts, proving that this is how John was killed. I now call on Mr. Hank Bauer, the forensic investigator in charge of the case, to testify."

A man with dark glasses and a brown suit gets up in the courtroom and begins to testify after taking the oath.

"Mr. Hank, how many years have you been investigating crimes like this?" Mr. Egghead asks.

"Nearly thirty years," he answers.

"And how many cases with similar characteristics have you investigated?"

"Over two hundred."

"Over two hundred… And this explanation I just gave here about the path the victim took while being hit is correct?"

"Yes, that's correct! As well as my report."

"Could you give us a broader explanation of what position the murderer was in and what material was used?"

Mr. Hank gets up and reenacts how the murderer struck the victim.

"Mr. Hank, explain something to us. Could a man of your height be able to leave marks like these on the wall?"

"No."

"Why?"

"The person would have to measure between 5'2 and 5'7. I'm 5'9."

"And did you check the height of all the residents, including children, employers, and employees of Yellowhammer?"

"Yes."

"And what can you tell us about it?"

"The only people with the corresponding height to leave blood splatters like these are Nora Bailey and Eliza Bailey. But, as we know, Eliza was with her mother in town when it all happened, as well as the twins, Asher and Bob, leaving only Nora." Mr. Hank answers.

"Thank you, Mr. Hank," Mr. Egghead says, facing the courtroom now. "You see, the only person present at Yellowhammer with the height corresponding to that of John Bailey's killer was her, Nora Bailey." Mr. Egghead points to me and continues, "All others were excluded from the investigation because they did not fit with the physical specificities that would generate this evidence. Mr. Hank, with this evidence, what did you conclude?"

"That it was an intentional homicide, motivated by passionate reasons."

"And why did you come to that conclusion?"

"The killer continued to strike after the victim was already dead."

"Which explains the sea of blood we can see all over the room, correct?"

"Precisely."

"Did you send the victim's body to be exhumed, Mr. Hank?"

"Yes, we found wood fragments mixed with the skull in the exhumation. These fragments would have come off the murder weapon." Mr. Hank explained.

"Could you say what kind of wood was found?"

"Yes, white cedar. This type of wood is often used to make baseball bats."

"And did you ever find out if there were any baseball bats on the Yellowhammer farm?" Mr. Egghead asked.

"Yes, the twins, Asher and Bob, had clubs made of this wood. But Bob's bat disappeared on the day of the incident, which means that the killer possibly took the murder weapon from the brothers' bedroom moments before attacking the victim." Mr. Hank answered.

"And you've found more evidence that brings us closer to Nora's guilt, haven't you, Mr. Hank?"

"Let's just say the investigation started when we discovered Nora's fingerprints on the Baileys' headboard. Then we also found shoes that could only have been hers, thrown at the back of the house where the crime occurred, along with a witch's hat, which was part of her Halloween costume. The costume was found under the Baileys' bed at the crime scene.

"Thank you for your enlightening, Mr. Hank. No further questions."

Mr. Hank, with his square bottle glasses and a brown suit, gets up, cleans his glasses without hurry, looks at me with a question mark in his eyes, and sits next to the jury.

Ms. O'Brien and I hold hands as Mr. Egghead continues to talk.

"Your Honor, as we heard from Mr. Hank, an expert on the subject, the killer enters the Baileys' property, goes to the twins' room, takes one of the baseball bats that would be the murder weapon, and goes to Mr. John and Elizabeth's room. There, finding the victim sleeping, the killer begins to deliver several blows to the victim's head, cracking his skull and leaving him with no possibility of reaction. Even after the victim's death, the killer gives more blows, leaving the scene of the crime covered in blood, which denotes that it is an intentional, passionate crime. Now I ask you, ladies and gentlemen, who in all of Yellowhammer would have any reason for such savagery?"

Mr. Egghead looks at Hank before he continues to speak.

"Renowned, experienced experts like Mr. Hank's went after any disagreement that could have arisen between John and one of his employees, but nothing was found. John was a man admired by everyone around him, and he had no quarrels with anyone. When questioned, everyone said they were satisfied with their work conditions and the salaries offered by John. So who could have done something like that to such a good, worthy man? I answer you—Nora! This monster that has been free all this time mocks us, John's family, this courtroom, our laws, and justice."

Mr. Egghead looks like he's going to explode. He's inflamed like the devil, and while he's talking, he's squirming so much that it gives us the impression that he could go into cardiac arrest at any moment. His talkativeness resembles that of a pastor taken by the Holy Spirit, transforming the entire courtroom into a church in a state of grace. Ms. O'Brien, my uncles, and I watched him with detachment, hoping that Judge Cassidy wasn't falling for his exaggeration.

Mr. Egghead starts again, saying, "Even considering all those present at the Yellowhammer farm, there is one more issue. Nora was the last to show up at the crime scene, so I ask you, where was she? What was she doing at the time of the crime? We know she didn't sleep at home, as usual. We also know she had taken a shower and changed her clothes before arriving at the crime scene. And you know what's even weirder? Nora was not used to taking a shower in the morning. We gathered this information through the various testimonials of the residents and employees of the Yellowhammer farm. She had a strict routine there and never did anything outside what she was used to. So I ask you again, why, on the day of the crime, Nora breaks the rules and decides to do everything differently? Had she gone to dispose of the murder weapon and wipe the blood off her clothes and body?"

After Mr. Egghead forces an eloquent silence, he continues, "Nora mocks justice! And I'm not the one saying this; it's the facts. Nora's shoes were found at the back of the victim's house, and we all know Nora didn't live in that house. She lived with her uncle Bruce and her cousin Andrew in another house, many feet away. The self-made Halloween costume hat was found at the crime scene, under the victim's bed, and her fingerprints were on Mr. and Mrs. Bailey's headboard. With all this evidence, we should ask ourselves how Nora spent all this time waiting for the trial in freedom. I leave you to answer these questions."

Mr. Egghead looks triumphant. He finishes formulating his accusation and looks at Judge Cassidy with an air of satisfaction, feeling victorious.

"That's all, Your Honor," He finally says.

After Mr. Egghead sits down, Ms. O'Brien prepares for the defense. As expected, Elizabeth made it look like I was responsible for Uncle John's death. Mr. Egghead's evidence is my fingerprints on the bed, the shoes at the back of the house, and the hat at the crime scene. I question who forged this evidence. My fingerprints could be found all over that house. I was the one who helped to assemble that bed, who cleaned all the things there, nothing more natural than them finding my fingertips in every corner.

Ms. O'Brien stands up, asking Judge Cassidy's permission, and starts to speak, "Ladies and gentlemen, I would like to start by talking about how evil humans are. Humans, in some cases, reach their greatest obscenity. What would you think if I said that Nora, this girl here, after losing her parents, and having nowhere to go except at Yellowhammer with her relatives, instead of receiving proper care, was subjugated to working conditions analogous to slavery? Nora lived in a critical situation at the Yellowhammer farm. She worked for the right to eat and sleep, and that was all. Living there, at sixteen, she had to cook, clean, sew, and work in the fields without any pay or benefits. Nora couldn't go to school, she couldn't go out, she didn't have friends, she didn't receive the same treatment as her cousins, and she worked day and night taking care of the farm's chores. When she tried to run away, she was threatened by this woman present here, Elizabeth Bailey!"

At that moment, everyone looks at Elizabeth in the courtroom. I had avoided looking at her since the first day of the trial, but as Ms. O'Brien spoke, I looked at her too.

Everyone who lived or worked there knew that Elizabeth kept Nora in an unworthy situation, but they didn't do anything to stop the abuse."

Then Mr. Egghead interrupts Ms. O'Brien, "I object. The one in a trial here is Nora. Mrs. O'Brien is making serious accusations against a woman whose character is impeccable. This is inadmissible, Your Honor."

"Denied. Ms. O'Brien, please continue."

"Yes, Your Honor." Ms. O'Brien said before turning to the audience again. "The fact is, ladies and gentlemen, Nora lived in these conditions for a long time. She was treated like a slave after losing her parents and everything she had. Nothing can reverse this. And yet, Nora was cowardly accused of a crime she did not commit."

Again, Mr. Egghead interrupts Ms. O'Brien impatiently, "If that's true, it just shows us that Nora would have another reason to commit these crimes, Mrs. O'Brien."

"For the first time, we agree, Mr. Smith." Ms. O'Brien said. "Nora would have reasons to commit this crime, indeed. However, having a reason is not the same as committing a crime, is it?"

"No, we don't agree on anything. I'm just saying that your allegations are so absurd that they collaborate to further reinforce your client's guilt, and it's almost a joke," Mr. Egghead says.

"If you didn't get so hasty and manage to respect when it's my turn to speak, you would understand that I am just getting started."

Ms. O'Brien walks over to Judge Cassidy and delivers Elizabeth's indictment protocol with testimony from half of

Yellowhammer employees that confirms my mistreatment before she goes on.

"I've just handed over Elizabeth's indictment for all her crimes while Nora was under her custody. In this indictment, part of the employees of the Yellowhammer farm report having seen everything I just described. But moving on, to alleviate Mr. Smith's anxiety because he can't hear a woman finish what she has to say before interrupting her, I want to ask him if he found the murder weapon. Did you, Mr. Smith?"

Enraged, Mr. Egghead says, "No."

"How can you be so sure that Nora was responsible for the killing of John Bailey when you don't even have the murder weapon in your hands? This only points out that this accusation was hastily made with almost no materiality, as if someone wanted it to be done soon with it… as if someone had already chosen who to blame. Elizabeth, as everyone knows, is an influential woman who would benefit financially if her husband ceased to exist."

"I object, Your Honor." Mr. Egghead screams in court.

Judge Cassidy acquiesces and reprimands Ms. O'Brien, "Granted. Ms. O'Brien, save your accusations for another trial."

Complacent, Ms. O'Brien apologizes before continuing her exposition, "Well, ladies and gentlemen… I want to ask you a question. Could Nora, who worked like no one else in that farmhouse, have left fingerprints all over the rooms?"

Mr. Egghead interrupts again, "Ms. O'Brien, please! The lady judge just said there is no evidence that Nora worked under those conditions, as you claim. If you have nothing for the defense, it would be best to remain silent and prevent Elizabeth from suing you for moral damages."

"Mr. Smith, unlike you, I know how to do my job. I had all the cleaning objects at the Baileys' properly examined, and you know what they have in common? They all have Nora's fingerprint on them and no one else's. Here is the report."

Ms. O'Brien delivers the forensic report with my fingerprints and photos of the inspected objects to the judge. Then she exhibits footage of the farm's outside area that shows me doing my chores.

"Here, you can see Nora working outside the Yellowhammer farm. This footage comes from the farm's security system. It would be great if we could get access to the camera footage of Yellowhammer's main house, we would have the crime solved! But the main camera was broken even before Nora came to live there. But these images show Nora going back and forth in the field when she should be at school or doing anything else. She's clearly doing roles that shouldn't be hers. All of this tells us that Nora's fingerprints could be found in any room in the house where the crime took place, as she was working there."

"And how do you explain Nora's shoes in the back of the Baileys' house or the fancy hat she was wearing at the crime scene?" Mr. Egghead questions.

"Someone could have implanted this evidence there, someone with influence, someone who wanted to take the focus off herself. Someone who knew what was going on there," Ms. O'Brien answers.

Mr. Egghead sneers at Ms. O'Brien sarcastically, "Mrs. O'Brien, you must agree that this is a conspiracy theory. I presented relevant evidence for the clarification of the case. What Mrs. O'Brien just said does not prove anything; it does not exclude the solid materiality of the accusation. She did her job, but it was not enough. Let's not sugar the pill. Nora, unhappy with all the changes in her life, with her emotional temper disrupted due to the medication and her bestial aggression, decided to go to the Baileys' room to get revenge for a lousy reason. She was mad she wasn't taken to a Halloween celebration... For not being suitable for country life... For having enjoyed killing her own parents by poisoning... It doesn't matter! You know very well that a psychopath needs no reason to kill an innocent. The fact is, with no mercy and a lot of coldness, Nora ended the life of an honorable man. How do you explain the evidence collected by Mr. Hank, in which the killer's height coincides with Nora's stature?"

"Thank you, Mr. Smith. I was about to get there." After taking a report from the table to Judge Cassidy, Ms. O'Brien addresses the Jury, "Ladies and gentlemen, I have just given the judge another forensic report from the crime scene that clarifies how the analysis of the killer's height was not done with due care. Sorry to say, but Mr. Hank was wrong, as he was in three other cases five and seven years ago and helped put two innocent people behind bars. Today, they have been able to reverse that and are now free, thanks to the trial being reviewed. In his report, Mr. Hank stated that the killer struck the victim on the head while standing by the bed. It so happens that this report I gave Judge Cassidy says something quite different. It says the killer climbed onto the bed and mounted the victim, causing the victim to wake up and try to free himself by moving on the bed. This caused the blood spatter trails, with no linear order, as Mr. Hank showed us. New information obtained by our expertise is that the killer's height is almost impossible to distinguish. Yet, the killer's weight and body shape are more important than his height. Nora would never be able to mount her uncle and dominate him, for John Bailey was much bigger and heavier than Nora. In this case, this evidence of height has no relevance whatsoever."

Ms. O'Brien turns to Judge Cassidy and mentions that she is done for now. And so, Mr. Egghead goes to Judge Cassidy.

"Your Honor, I would now like to call the victim's brother to the stand, Bruce Bailey."

Judge Cassidy acquiesces. Mr. Egghead looks at me with a sarcastic smile on his face.

Uncle Bruce enters. He's visibly off-balance, like a dog amid the roar of fireworks. His gaze is low, and his eyes are almost hidden under a red cap, with the brim folded down his forehead. He walks in and doesn't even dare to look at me. He looks at Elizabeth, and at that moment, I turn and look at her too. She's there, dressed in black, like an impenetrable rock, her chin arched up as if she's hovering. Above all, she seems untouchable. She exudes a tyrannical air from the most underground places of the human soul.

Mr. Egghead interrogates my uncle, "Mr. Bruce Bailey, you were at your house the night before the crime, as stated in the statement you gave to Mr. Hank, right?"

Uncle Bruce responds with a downcast gaze while seeking Elizabeth's eyes, "Yes, sir!"

Mr. Egghead continues, "Is it true that the accused lived in the same house as you and your son?"

"Yes, it's true," Uncle Bruce says.

"Here in your statement, you reported that you heard Nora yelling at your son Andrew in front of the house at dusk?"

"Yes."

"Could you describe your son's illness, Mr. Hank?"

"He's not a normal kid. He's a little late in his development."

"You mean that he has microcephaly, right, Mr. Bruce?"

"Right, I couldn't remember the name of his defect."

"Of his condition, you mean?"

"Yes, Mr. Smith! The boy has microcephaly, just like you said," Uncle Bruce answers in an angry tone.

"And has it been difficult for you to take care of the boy?"

"Yes, it has always been very difficult, but Elizabeth is like a mother to him. She cares for the boy as if he were her son. She helps me a lot!"

"And what was his relationship with Nora like?"

At that moment, Uncle Bruce begins to exchange glances with Elizabeth, and he begins to respond as if following a script.

"Nora never cared much for the boy, he always tried to make friends with her, but she always left the boy talking to himself."

"And the night Nora yelled at your son, did you ever try to stop her from doing that?"

"I tried, but she had already left when I got to the door."

"So you saw her run away?' Where did she go?"

"I saw Nora run into the woods."

"And after that, did you see her again?"

"No, after that, she never came home."

"So that night, you didn't see Nora again at her house?"

"No sir, I would have heard her return if she had done that. The wooden floor of the house always creaks when people are walking around it.

"And when did you see Nora again?" Mr. Egghead asks.

"Just the following morning."

"The day your brother's body was discovered?"

"That's right."

"That's all, Mr. Bruce. Thank you very much! May God comfort your heart and the hearts of your family members."

When Mr. Egghead dismisses Uncle Bruce, Ms. O'Brien intervenes and requests a turn with the witness. At that moment, Mr. Egghead almost faints and starts to be scandalized, saying that this wouldn't be possible, that this would not happen at all, and that the request was absurd. Mr. Egghead's objection to Ms. O'Brien's interrogation arouses great curiosity in Judge Cassidy.

"Mr. Bruce, would you be so kind as to answer just a few questions for Nora's attorney, Ms. O'Brien?"

And before Mr. Egghead and Elizabeth stop him, Uncle Bruce says *yes*. At that moment, Mr. Egghead turns to Elizabeth shaking his head negatively, and he whispers to her that this could be the end for them in the case.

Ms. O'Brien approaches Uncle Bruce, greets him, and politely starts asking him some questions. And that's when the trial begins to take a crazy turn. I didn't know all the details of the case, Uncles Ted and Mark thought it best to deprive me of several defense findings to protect myself, so I could have a "normal" life—forgetting everything from my past. I was as surprised as everyone else in that courtroom when Ms. O'Brien started interrogating Uncle Bruce, and all pieces of the puzzle began to come together in my head.

"Mr. Bruce, you claim you didn't see Nora until the morning they found your brother John's body, correct?"

"Yes."

"Didn't you look for Nora all this time?' Weren't you worried about her being alone and lost in the woods at night?"

"I thought she was with her cousins at the big house."

"But you knew they were in town for the Halloween celebration, didn't you?"

"Yes, but I thought they could be back by then."

"Did you hear the car arrive?"

"Yes, ma'am."

"Do you remember the Time?"

"No, ma'am, I remember it was late at night."

"You didn't hear Nora arrive, but you heard the noise of your brother John's car arriving late at night... Did you leave the house that night or that morning, Mr. Bruce?"

"No, of course not! I stayed there all night."

"Okay ... You had your senses awake to know that Nora had not arrived, and your brother did. Mr. Bruce, did you sleep well that night?"

"No, I didn't sleep well."

"Why?"

"I had a lot on my mind," he answers.

"What sort of things were you thinking of, Mr. Bruce?" Ms. O'Brien asks.

Uncle Bruce is silent for a long time and then replies, "I don't remember now."

Ms. O'Brien then asks to play some more videos in court for Judge Cassidy, who grants her the request. Ms. O'Brien puts the first video, and we can see the date of the murder in the corner of the screen.

"As you can see, this recording is from when John Bailey was killed. We took the same camera that sits next to the big house that had filmed Nora working weeks before, and we've restored the archive of footage from the day of the murder. The file had been criminally damaged. These are the images that someone attempted to hide from this investigation."

As we watch the video recording on the screen, Ms. O'Brien says, "As the video shows, this is the moment when John Bailey's car arrives in Yellowhammer. We can see by the car's headlight reflection. And if we fast-forward the video to exactly one hour and forty-three minutes later, we'll see a man in a jacket and cap walk by holding shoes and a hat, just like the one Nora made." Ms. O'Brien pauses the video, then goes to Uncle Bruce and asks clearly and directly, "Are you sure you didn't leave the house that night, Mr. Bruce?"

"No! Of course not! Do you think I don't know what you're trying to imply? Are you crazy, you bitch?"

"I'm not implying anything." Ms. O'Brien turns to Mr. Egghead. "A picture's worth a thousand words, isn't it, Mr. Smith?"

Mr. Egghead, who once boasted like a wild beast at anything Ms. O'Brien said, now lowers his head and embitters the most shameful silence of his career as a man of "justice."

But at the same time, abruptly and without them being able to stop it, Uncle Bruce advances toward Ms. O'Brien.

"Hey! Hey! I'm talking to you, you bitch! Do you think you can frame me? Do you know who I am? Do you think you can come here and point your finger at me? You're nothing but a shitty lawyer! I'll finish you off, do you hear me? I'll crush you!"

Uncle Bruce reaches for Ms. O'Brien, who ducks and shrinks as he screams. Two officers go to him and contain him.

Judge Cassidy screams, "Arrest this man! Arrest this man!"

The officers handcuff Uncle Bruce.

While Uncle Bruce is handcuffed, Ms. O'Brien interrupts the judge and asks her to wait for her to finish. Judge Cassidy denies it and orders her offices to arrest Uncle Bruce immediately.

"I've seen everything I needed to see."

"Allow me, then, just to conclude, Your Honor." Ms. O'Brien insists.

"As you wish, but be quick about it."

All of us in the courtroom felt cathartic after the uproar. We were all in shock, tired, and not knowing what else to expect. The people who were there could not believe what they were seeing. Mr. Egghead had his hands over his face.

Elizabeth, now wearing sunglasses, was looking for a way out of there, staring at the exit doors. As Ms. O'Brien took photos of the murder weapon from an envelope on her desk, "Here is, your honor, the murder weapon! Police found it hidden in Mr. Bruce's house's trapdoor yesterday. It had the victim's blood and the killer's fingerprints, Bruce Bailey."

Ms. O'Brien delivers the photos to Judge Cassidy, along with some papers with DNA tests that prove that the blood found on the bat was the victim's and the fingerprints were Bruce Bailey's, leaving no doubt that he was the killer.

"Ladies and gentlemen, as you can all see, Bruce Bailey is the real killer of John Bailey, his brother. But it doesn't end here. Alabama justice has yet to discover who else is involved in this horrendous crime."

At that moment, Ms. O'Brien glares at Elizabeth, who gets up and hurries out of the courtroom.

"It is not always easy to determine who is to blame because of economic power, influences, and agreements with important people. Innocent people end up paying for their crimes. So be suspicious! Be suspicious when they quickly point the finger at someone, when they choose their criminal, when they condemn a person for nothing, denying this person the right of being innocent until proven guilty. The accuser may be the real criminal based on who they decide to blame."

Rectification. That was the word in my head when I walked out of the courtroom on the tenth day of the trial. Uncle Bruce was arrested, Elizabeth indicted, and Mr. Egghead walked out with his tail between his legs. All that was missing was the media's apology so that I could have my life back and people would look at me as a human being.

But the hours following Uncle Bruce's arrest were one of frightening silence, the echo of emptiness, nothingness from all the media. It made me understand more about how this game worked, which had nothing to do with transmitting information. It had to do with sides, like the sides of a coin—heads and tails. All newspapers had already chosen their side. Retraction is too expensive for them, who have chosen to defend dark political interests rather than honor.

Unlike what I expected, Bruce's arrest got a small note on the last page of the newspaper. Something quite different from what was portrayed about me when the accusations started. That injustice was just one of the many I suffered. It is possible that my goal of seeing justice triumph may never come true and that I could still be surprised on the last day of the trial by the announcement of my arrest. Moderation and modesty have never been enemies of wisdom; perhaps the best thing to do at this moment is to wait for oblivion. If they cannot acknowledge the truth, better forget about the lie, so little by little I can breathe again, relieved.

Chapter Six

The Verdict

Near the entrance to the Montgomery Courthouse, the press, this time with a reduced team, awaits us, asking for a statement.

Accompanied by my parents, Ted and Mark, I pass them, but a few steps ahead, I stop saying that I wanted to talk this time. My parents are reticent about the idea, but realizing how important it is to me, they allow it.

"I don't know what awaits me in there today; there have been many obstacles and suffering so far. I've had my life brutally ripped from me these past few months. I've lived through a nightmare that you will never understand. I hope the truth soon reaches everyone and I can have my life back, even with the open wounds that are now part of me. I am innocent! I swear it wasn't me! I'm fighting to get them to see this, feel this… The real culprits began to appear, and I'm sure that when you have all the pieces of this story in place, you will see that you were deceived and that I am the victim of a perverse plot orchestrated by evil people with a lot of power. Thank you."

"Nora, the accusations against you are still quite terrible. Are you confident?" A journalist asks.

"One thing my father always taught me is that you can never lose hope. That's all I have," I answer.

"We know that your uncle was arrested yesterday in court. Is he guilty of the other crimes you are being accused of? Another journalist asks.

"Yes," I answer.

"Nora, do you think you'll be cleared of all the accusations against you?"

"I hope so."

"What would you say to the prosecution that charged you with all these crimes?"

"May they turn criminals into convicts, not innocent people."

"Thank you, Nora!"

My parents, Ted and Mark, hold my hand as I enter the courthouse. I soon notice that something has changed in everyone's eyes. They look at me as a human being now, with politeness, perhaps even a certain embarrassment—like when we find out we were wrong about something or someone for a long time.

As I wait for Judge Cassidy to arrive, I tell myself, "The only thing I can do now is to keep myself calm, my head clear until the end."

Mr. Egghead arrives late. This man, who was always a bellicose moralist, who looked down on everyone with disdain and pride, now reappears as a modest and humble being. Perhaps now he gets it that he and his people are targets of justice. This time, impunity will not be victorious, and he will suffer the consequences of the injustice he instilled in me.

Then Judge Cassidy arrives, "Everyone, please stand."

As soon as she starts the trial, she invites Mr. Egghead to initiate my trial for killing my grandparents. To me, this is perhaps the most unjust accusation. So it is surprising to me when Mr. Egghead categorically approaches Judge Cassidy.

"Your Honor, I, Kurt Smith, representing the prosecution of Montgomery, came to withdraw the accusation that Nora Bailey killed her grandparents, Tony and Maria Bell. The prosecution reassessed the evidence in this case and found it insufficient to proceed with the prosecution. Accordingly, the Montgomery District Attorney and the state of Alabama drop this charge and await the verdict for the other two cases in which Nora Bailey was accused."

I listen to it all in disbelief, with my mouth slightly opened.

"Is Egghead really dropping the charges?" I ask my attorney. My heart beats fast, my hands tighten around Ms. O'Brien's, and I can barely contain myself. I feel so pleased. I feel like singing, dancing, jumping, and running. It could all end today, and I would have my life back. At that moment, I feel I might win and prove my innocence. The whole world would know it; Nora Bailey is innocent.

Mr. Egghead turns to the Jury and appeals for my conviction with a few words, "Ladies and gentlemen, I appreciate your patience during these days. Your presence so far has been of paramount importance and revives the fulfillment of the precepts of this house. I ask you one last favor while considering your decision. Remember the word of the Lord, *Beware of false prophets who come to you in sheep's clothing, but inwardly they are ravening wolves,* Matthew 7:15. Don't be fooled by appearances. May God guide you!"

Without realizing what he was doing, as he spoke, Mr. Egghead distorted the word of God so that the jury would understand that a young woman, a girl like me, could pass for a lamb while being a big bad wolf. It so happens that by appealing to this, he was speaking of himself. He was the false prophet, the man covered by a mantle of morals and good customs who commits various crimes and sins under the pretext of holiness. *Mr. Smith* is the real wolf who uses the instruments of justice to condemn innocent people in exchange for money and power.

Meanwhile, Ms. O'Brien prepares for her final speech by heading to the bench. With her text written in hand, she looks at everyone, and before she starts reading what she spent the night writing, she tears up the speech and speaks from her heart.

"I had here in my hands the final speech, as is the norm, at the end of a trial. It turns out that this trial is not like the others. It wasn't fair from the beginning because it's not fair to turn a victim into a criminal, a child into a murderer, and suggest that she should pay for her sins. For more than three hundred and sixty-five days, Elizabeth, Nora's legal guardian, was a central figure in indicting all the crimes that Nora Bailey has been accused of. She, and the Montgomery District Attorney, are responsible for ruining Nora's life by falsely pointing to her and telling the world that she was responsible for the deaths of her parents, Giovanna and Otto Bailey, her uncle John Bailey, and her grandparents, Maria and Tony Bell. Today, after so long, after this girl had to face deep pain alone, I ask you to do justice. I ask you to give Nora Bailey her life back. I ask you to let the world know she is not a murderer; she is not the monster the tabloids say. I ask you to help have the real culprits held accountable for their lies."

At that moment, Mr. Egghead loses all the coloration of his face and swallows his saliva.

"Ladies and Gentlemen, I greatly appreciate the service you provided during these judgment days." Ms. O'Brien goes on. "I understand that it was not easy being here every day, and I am grateful to you for the time you spent and the care you took in analyzing the evidence so that we could get to the truth of the facts. After all these days of listening to the depositions and gathering the evidence, now is the time for you, the jury, to decide. This is a serious task, what is being discussed here is the life of a great girl, and it is in your hands to give back what should never have been taken from her. Today, you have the possibility right the wrongs or join the side of the real criminals. That's what it's about now. All the evidence points to her innocence. We have no doubts about what happened. When the lies started, the liars knew what they were doing. They knew what would happen to Nora. Until then, they only knew that she was innocent and that everything they created was an absurd lie that would destroy Nora's life. The world believed this lie. The world saw a monster in a girl without parents, family, and friends because it was easier. I'm counting on you to show the world who Nora really is. I'm counting on you to give Nora her life back. May the truth set us all free."

This is when Judge Cassidy addresses the Jury, "Did you come to an agreement?"

"Not yet."

"I'm sorry, but I must ask that you do."

"We're not getting anywhere," The spokesperson says. "We're at an impasse."

"I don't care. If someone is resisting, talk and get somewhere," Judge Cassidy said.

"I'm sorry, Your Honor." The spokesperson said.

"Don't feel sorry! What's the count?"

"Six to six."

"Talk for another thirty minutes and bring me a verdict."

Judge Cassidy calls for a thirty-minute break until the jury gets to a verdict. At this point, I look at the jury, trying to identify who are the six people who voted against me.

"Are they with Elizabeth? What's going on?" I feel between heaven and hell. A little while ago, I already felt the winds of freedom rushing through me. This impasse puts me in front of doubt again, a feeling that has permeated all my days so far.

Outside of the courthouse, my parents and I wait apprehensively. Ms. O'Brien walks past and reassures us, telling us not to worry. I see Mr. Egghead talking to the Jury Spokesperson next to the bathroom, and I think it's strange. Still, the Spokesperson seems to dodge Mr. Egghead's advances and quickly passes into the inner area where the entire Jury is. My dad, Ted, gets angry and moves to go there, but we manage to stop him in time.

"Calm down! Nothing can go wrong now. Let's trust Ms. O'Brien, Judge Cassidy and wait. There's nothing left for us to do."

"Listen to Nora, baby," my dad Mark says. "We're almost done. Soon, we'll be free. Soon we will be a happy family."

With great gratitude, I turn to them, "We are already a happy family. You are everything to me! Thanks for supporting me this far."

We hug and hang around there, trying to distract ourselves. But time passes slowly. The minute hand takes an eternity to complete a turn of the clock. I feel the weight of those last few days—it feels like a decade…The days, hours, minutes, and seconds have crossed me so that I think my age no longer corresponds to my experiences in life. It makes me understand that time is my greatest asset over my enemies. If freedom beckons me, I won't waste another second, not a thousandth of time if I have a chance. I'll turn the milliseconds into minutes, hours into days, days into months, months into years, and years into centuries. I will live my journey without anything that can make me forget that my time will be spent being free. And nothing and no one will be able to put bars on my dreams and say that I can't do what I want. From now on, I am free, inside and beyond me, towards eternity.

I made a pact with myself at that moment—I would be happy every day. So I'll trouble anyone whose simple joy of material things inflicts poverty and indifference on the world. Maybe I'm naive in saying this; maybe dreaming of freedom like this is only possible because I'm close to losing it in this courtroom. Perhaps dreaming of freedom itself is a mistake, an offense. But once the head experiences being free, it no longer matters where the body ends up.

Ms. O'Brien approaches us, breathing heavily, looks us in the eyes, and says, "Ready? It is time."

We look at each other, take a deep breath, and hold hands, telling Ms. O'Brien we are ready. She leads us back to the courthouse. Before we can go inside, she grabs me by the arm.

"Can I give you a hug, Nora?" She asks me.

With my heart racing and the lids of my eyes fluttering, I say *yes*, and Ms. O'Brien gives me a tight, motherly hug. I look at her, and her eyes are clouded with tears.

We all go back into the courtroom and wait for another ten interminable minutes until Judge Cassidy arrives. My legs tremble, my breathing is heavy, my muscles are out of control, and my nervousness makes my body shake. Ms. O'Brien put her hand on my arm.

"Look at me! This ends right now. It will be alright; you will be acquitted."

I try to trust what she says, but my body doesn't obey me. It continues to tremble without my being able to control it. At this moment, the nervousness is so great that I can't contain my body, and a bit of urine leaks on my underwear before Judge Cassidy starts to speak. My senses go haywire. I try to concentrate all my strength to stay conscious, even though my eyes are hazy with the bright white light of the courtroom.

Judge Cassidy flips through some papers, nods, and gets up to address everyone, "Please stand. I have here the jury decision." Judge Cassidy begins reading the sentence. "Case number LM2016/2606, Nora Bailey against the state of Alabama, for the poisoning of her parents Giovanna and Otto Bailey, this jury finds Nora not guilty."

Ms. O'Brien squeezes my hand while I listen and vibrate in silence. A miracle was happening.

Judge Cassidy goes on, "In regards to case number LM2016/2607, Nora Bailey against the state of Alabama, for the brutal murder of John Bailey with a baseball bat, the jury finds the defendant not guilty."

Confirming the miracle of the jury changing their minds in my favor, they acquit me for the accusation of murdering my uncle. At that point, I was astonished.

"Jury members, these are the verdicts. Is anyone who does not agree with the verdicts that have been read here?" Numb and in disbelief, I watch as the jury agrees with the verdict. "Well, I thank you for your service to this court. I am also immensely grateful to say that, Nora Bailey, you are free from all charges."

My body, weakened by the emotions that ran through me, caused me to fall into the chair as I let out a cry. It was as if my soul was crying. When I collapsed, Ms. O'Brien promptly came to my side and stayed by my side until I could recover.

It's over. I, Nora Bailey, am free to go on with my life. I'm innocent in the eyes of justice.

I feel like I am being born again. I look at my parents, Ted and Mark, and they look at me, smiling. Outside the courtroom, we held each other for a long time, not saying a single word. Everything had already been said through our eyes. I couldn't stop thinking about everything I would do from that moment on. Hurricane Nora was behind us. I can finally be someone normal, or at least I can try.

I was so beside myself that anything made me cry. I couldn't believe it was over, and I was crying now from happiness. I couldn't wait to get out of that place, return to California and start from scratch. A new life for a new Nora. In this new version, I don't get hurt anymore, and I don't let anyone else do it to me. I'm free and grateful for my life and my parents' lives. Common problems don't make me lose sleep. The food has more flavors, and birthdays and special dates are celebrated. I'll remember my late parents affectionately, and they'll receive my prayers wherever they are. There is room to hope for a better future that will flourish. There is room for me to believe in myself and trust others. There is day and night, the sky, the moon, and the stars. There's sea, deserts, forests, rivers, rainbows, animals, insects, nature... there is my nature, which is perfect, like everyone else's. All this is possible now. I can be me in this world—and that's a lot. It should be enough for me.

"Nora, would you like to go somewhere to celebrate?" Dad Mark asks enthusiastically.

I take a deep breath and reply, "No! I just want to go home."

"If that's what you want, Ted can cook for you, right, baby?"

"Really? I guess I'd rather stop by any fast-food place to get hamburgers and fries," I say, and we laugh.

"You two are just not yet ready to understand the sophistication of the dishes I cook."

"Yes, my love, you're right!" Dad Mark says. "We are the ones who have an underdeveloped palate. Your food is great. It is so sophisticated that indigestion is immediate. We eat and go to the bathroom," he teases.

"We can even let you cook dinner, dad, but you need to let the hospital know in case of any complications, ok?"

"Fine... Fine... You'll get diddlysquat when you ask me to cook something for you. I won't go into the kitchen even," Dad Ted says, annoyed by our teasing.

"We appreciate that, baby. Thank you."

"Yeah, we're never going to ask you to cook. Do not worry!"

"You guys will beg for my food one of these days, I'm sure!"

We all laugh.

Before heading outside the courtroom, we decide to turn on our cell phones, and a shower of notifications starts to pop across the screen. Several media outlets are reporting the outcome of the trial. The media reported that I was acquitted but implied that the trial had not been fair. They stuck to the rhetoric that the prosecution backed down precisely in the case where they had the most evidence of my guilt, the case of my grandparents' death. The internet was also in an uproar. My name was among the most popular topics, and there were many hate messages, threats, and fake news.

Perhaps these days are one of the most dangerous. We live in a time of lies. Lies are created in an absurd amount, and the speed and reach they have are frightening. The world is becoming a minefield, and the terrifying thing is that few people are truly concerned about it.

I hope it cools down soon, and they forget about me. That's what I want—to be forgotten. I want the new Nora not to worry about the lies they made about the Nora of the past. Time will once again save me from the bad guys; soon, I won't be in new news anymore. Lies are fed by things that are new and interesting. Soon I will cease to be interesting to them and disappear, and everything will be spectacularly simple, wonderfully normal.

Stepping outside the courthouse, a crowd of people and journalists await us. A barricade was created in front of the main door of the Montgomery courthouse, where officers controlled who could and could not pass. The journalist I spoke to earlier before the trial asks us to let him photograph us together. So we position ourselves by the door for him to take pictures of us. My parents stood by my side. That was our family, our beautiful family, united and happy. I turn around and ask them to kiss. They do it after my insistence, and with that, more than one photographer takes a picture of it. Several flashes fire up in our direction. We started to find that amusing, dad Mark risks some poses in a joking tone, and we, at all times, are smiling—a sincere smile that shows who we are without hiding anything. We laugh like children, perfectly and happy, as if a beautiful sunny day had opened after a dark and terrible storm in our lives.

The Journalist takes a tape recorder out of his pocket and asks me, "Nora, could you answer some questions for me?"

I should say no and go home with my parents. But with all that joy, I couldn't say no to anyone.

"Sure," I say.

"How would you like to be seen now that you've been cleared?"

"I just want respect. Since this started, the media has portrayed me in a stupid and awful way."

"What would you say to the people who always believed in you?" The journalist asks.

"I would say *thank you*. Thanks so much for letting me prove my innocence."

"What are you going to do now that you're free?"

"Rebuild the life they stole from me."

"What would you say to the people who accused you?"

"I think I would say that convicting an innocent is the same as being an accomplice to a crime. You need evidence to convict someone, and when that doesn't happen, the best thing to do is wait in silence."

"What was it like to receive these accusations and see the case having such repercussions in the press?"

"It was very painful! I was portrayed as a monster. They made me lose precious time in my life, and many times I got hurt. I thought several times about giving up on life. In addition to irresponsibility, the press was criminal in some instances."

"And do you and your guardians intend to take any action in response to these cases, or is the matter closed for you?"

"I'd like to say it's closed, but the truth is just beginning to be revealed. My being acquitted is just the beginning; my lawyer has filed an indictment so that the real responsible people can pay for their crimes."

"Do you believe that the press will redeem itself?"

"I hope they do what's right. I've always looked forward to this and still have the same hope. I need to believe in a brighter future for me."

When the Journalist got ready to ask one more question, and we asked him to make sure it was the last one, a tall, strong white man broke through the police blockade and pushed some journalists away to get to us. The man carried a dark shadow and an uncontrolled fury. He managed to reach me and touch me with his empty gaze.

"Death to the impure!"

At that moment, the man pulls out a gun, cocks the hammer, and slams the cold steel of the weapon against my chest while I can feel my heart pounding in my forehead.

My arteries were pumping blood hard throughout my body. And then the man with his coldness and madness, pulls the trigger, the gun's hammer drops, and the bullet explodes in me.

I fall flat on the ground; the police restrain the shooter while my parents try to help me, screaming for help. I feel my flesh burning, the blood flooding my clothes, and consciousness leaving my body slowly. A flash opens, and in front of me, I recognize a friend. I look at it with a tender smile, and the closer it gets to me, the lighter I feel. Then, very sweetly, the moose kneels, lays his head on my chest, and I go with it toward my freedom in an eternal embrace.

I didn't want this hug to come so soon, but all life is brief, like a flash of time. Nothing was lost; nothing was in vain. When things have deteriorated, love is the only way out. Despite not knowing what it has accomplished, I have not given up on my ideal. Neither my words nor my story belongs to me, nor does my air, which now returns to the earth.

I don't know how this started. The page is empty now. Everything I said was true, except for what I made up. The end of the story, of my story, is the end of the whole world. But everything that ends begins again; life begins again. Words are stirred again, verbs dance, and all we want is...

To Continue

To Continue.

To Continue.

VALLENTINA TURMINA

Acknowledgment

I would like to start by thanking my mom, Vicktoria Túrmina, for supporting and encouraging me to write this book. I would also like to thank everyone on the team that helped me polish and publish this book. I am so happy and proud to have worked alongside so many amazing people!